THE INVISIBLE ENEMY

The Invisible Harry
illustrated by Abby Carter

The Invisible Day
illustrated by Abby Carter

Earthly Astonishments

Hannah and the Seven Dresses

Hannah's Collections

Marthe Jocelyn

•

The Invisible Enemy

illustrated by **Abby Carter**

D U T T O N   C H I L D R E N ' S   B O O K S   •   *New York*

Text copyright © 2002 by Marthe Jocelyn
Illustrations copyright © 2002 by Abby Carter

Library of Congress Cataloging-in-Publication Data
Jocelyn, Marthe.
The invisible enemy / by Marthe Jocelyn; illustrations by
Abby Carter.—1st ed.
p. cm.
Sequel to: The invisible Harry.
Summary: Sixth-grader Billie finds her life complicated when a cute boy from Montreal transfers to her school and her enemy, Alyssa, accidentally uses her vanishing powder.
ISBN 0-525-46831-5
[1. Science—Experiments—Fiction. 2. Schools—Fiction.
3. New York (N.Y.)—Fiction. 4. Canadian Americans—
Fiction. 5. Humorous stories.] I. Carter, Abby, ill.
PZ7.J579 Io 2002 [Fic]—dc21 2001028692

Published in the United States by Dutton Children's Books,
a division of Penguin Putnam Books for Young Readers
345 Hudson Street, New York, New York 10014
www.penguinputnam.com

Printed in USA
First Edition
1 3 5 7 9 10 8 6 4 2

CONTENTS

THE INVISIBLE ENEMY

1 • Brownie Brat

On the first day back to school after winter break, I was the only person who knew there was going to be a new boy in the sixth grade. Being the daughter of the school librarian has few benefits, but getting the occasional inside scoop is one of them.

This was my chance to make good on my New Year's Resolution Number One: Get more friends! I have a best friend, Hubert, but he's also pretty much my only friend. I had decided to make an impression on more of the world than just Hubert. I was going to find this new boy and be really nice and help him fit in, and he would be friends with Hubert and me and not with Alyssa.

Resolution Number Two was to stop letting Alyssa Morgan bother me so much. That one dissolved as soon as Hubert and I stepped into the courtyard. As she stood on the steps, passing around a box of brownies, my sworn enemy looked like a queen tossing crumbs from the castle tower. A typical Alyssa gesture—bribing the peasants in an effort to inspire devotion. Half the sixth grade crowded around her, munching chocolate and screaming praise, their breath puffing out in the cold air like steam on cocoa.

Crossing the yard, I looked around for a new face, but all I saw were familiar ones with full mouths.

"These are wicked good!" said Josh, still chewing, so it came out, *Ese ur icky goo!*

"You made these, Alyssa?" said Sarah. "They're awesome!"

"Get one, Hubert." Victor drooled brown slime.

"Oh, uh, no, maybe, I dunno," said Hubert, glancing at me. I could tell he was weighing the loyalty issue. But the brownies were Rocky Roads, with nuts and marshmallows plunked on top.

Alyssa waved the box under Hubert's nose. "Come on, Bertie. You don't need her permission."

"Thanks," he said, taking one.

Alyssa looked at me and smirked, like she'd won five points. Then she held the box in my direction. I admit, they smelled delicious. I fell for it and reached out.

"Oh, sorry." She snatched the box back, leaving my hand stranded in midair. "I don't seem to have enough for you."

There were at least five left. I saw them! My cheeks burned. Resolution Number Two was now crushed under my boots like old snow.

Alyssa hopped off the step and spun around on the toes of her silver boots, cackling.

I stood there like a dolt, hating her. Of course, if I use the word *hate*, my mother says it's as bad as swearing, and I should put ten cents in the Bad Word Jar.

Alyssa has been in my class every year from

kindergarten right up till now. In kindergarten, she bit me so hard her teeth made marks through my sweater. Now she bites just with words. She's so mean to Hubert, I could spit. Last year she stole his idea for the fifth-grade project and then just copied her work out of books, totally cheating.

Recently I've had a couple of good swipes at revenge, thanks to having a secret weapon. But it's so secret that Alyssa's not sure I'm to blame, and what's the fun in that? If I added up all the ten-centses I've spent on hating her, I'd have enough money to buy my own portable CD player.

"Here." Hubert broke his brownie and offered me half. Alyssa watched me in anticipation.

"I wouldn't eat that if it were the last food in New York City," I said loudly. "She probably didn't make them herself anyway. She bought them from a deli and just says they're hers."

"That's a stinking lie, Billie Stoner!" said Alyssa. "I did so make them!"

Good, her face had that hot, ugly look. I rolled my eyes in a superior kind of a way and caught sight of a boy leaning against the tree near the fence. Even though it was freezing, he was wearing only a bashed-up denim jacket. He had wild black hair and no hat and—oh—it must be him!

"Hey!" I announced, as casually as I could. "I guess that's the new boy in our class. The one my mother was telling me all about."

Alyssa clapped the lid on her brownie box. Everyone turned to stare at the stranger. Our school is small enough to welcome new blood like a gift at a vampire wedding. Of course, from across the yard, the new boy didn't know why he was suddenly the center of attention. He glanced behind him, but no one was there.

"Ohmigod, he's cute!" said Alyssa.

I totally agreed, only of course I didn't say so.

"He looks like a gypsy," said Alyssa. That was true, too, partly because of his dark hair and skin, but mostly because he didn't look American. He looked exotic and confident and—well, cute. He somehow managed to keep looking at us while we inspected him. I would have ducked my eyes in a second.

After a minute he pulled a chrome yo-yo out of his pocket and zipped it up and down a couple of times, not wearing gloves, of course. Then, with a casual flick, the yo-yo sailed above his head like a tiny, glittering spotlight before whooshing behind him and all the way back up again in front. He had executed a perfect Reach-for-the-Moon.

"Wow," said Hubert.

"Mighty!" gushed Josh, who'd been trying to master that move since September, when everyone seemed to get new yo-yos at the same time.

"Yep," I said, "that's him all right."

"What school was he at?" asked Josh.

"He's French," I said. "I mean, he talks French. From Montreal, Quebec."

Mouths dropped open all around me. Hubert gaped. I think he was hurt that I hadn't told him about the new boy. But how could I have explained about my secret plan to recruit him as a friend?

"I love his hair," said Alyssa.

Was he still watching us? I got a crick in my neck trying to see without turning to look.

"Why did he transfer in the middle of the year?" asked Megan.

"His mother is part of a teaching exchange at New York University," I said. "She's a professor of, um, French."

"Well, la-di-da. What's his name, you know-it-all?" asked Alyssa.

"He sure can handle a yo-yo," said Hubert, not even pretending not to look. The bell rang for class. The boy stuffed the yo-yo in his pocket and headed toward the school doors.

"His name is Jean-Pierre," I said in triumph. "Jean-Pierre de la Tutu or something. And I think we should say hello." But Alyssa beat me to it.

"Bon joor!" she shouted. "Bon joor!" She flipped a shining braid over her shoulder and waved as if the boy were a taxi driver. "Hey! You!" She used her fashion-model waggle to cross the yard. A parade of other kids followed. I shoved my fists in my pockets and watched Alyssa grab my new friend.

"Voolay-voo oon brownie? I've got lots left over!"

2 · The New Boy

The desks in our classroom are arranged in a sort of circle, so we all face each other. Mr. Donaldson had squeezed in an extra desk with the name *Jean-Pierre* printed on a card to match the others. I watched, steaming, while Alyssa guided the poor boy to his place as if he were blind.

"I speak English," I heard him say. "And I can see."

His voice was a bit husky, which made his accent sound like someone in a movie. He was even cuter close up, with hazely eyes and long lashes. Alyssa just kept standing there, staring at him. Her pal Megan leaned over and poked her to stop making a fool of herself.

"Take your seats, people. Settle down. Welcome back, everyone. I'd like to officially welcome our newcomer, Jean-Pierre de LaTour."

Jean-Pierre saluted and smiled a crooked smile. His desk was directly opposite mine, so I caught the main shine. Hubert is next to me, and Alyssa is three over, well out of smile range.

"You'll have plenty of time during the day to show Jean-Pierre how friendly New Yorkers can be." Mr. Donaldson looked around. "Ah, Hubert? Would you be Jean-Pierre's buddy for today?"

Hubert blushed and nodded at Jean-Pierre to introduce himself. In our class, it is well known that Hubert does not like to speak out loud. Especially not to strangers. Mr. D. picked him on purpose—an exercise in torture disguised as social encouragement.

"Show him around, make sure he finds the cafeteria and other essential facilities. . . ." Mr. Donaldson always calls the bathroom "the facilities."

Jean-Pierre nodded back at Hubert and spun his yo-yo like a top across his desk.

"Toys are not allowed in the classroom," said Mr. Donaldson, with a laser-beam squint. "Since it's your first day, I'll let you off with a warning." He laughed to try to show he was a nice guy, but we all knew he was dying to add that yo-yo to the collection of our treasures in his bottom drawer.

"All right then, listen up, people. We have a busy quarter ahead of us, with the first focus on your projects about medieval life. We have a couple of field trips coming up, starting this week—"

"Are we going on a school bus or the subway?" asked Josh.

"—with an excursion, on a school bus, to the Cloisters. That's Friday, leaving first thing. We'll be seeing a marvelous reconstruction of medieval architecture as well as—yes, Josh?"

"Do we have to bring lunch?"

"You'll need to bring a bag lunch, no glass bottles, no candy—yes, Josh?"

"Can we have soda, sir?"

"Yes, you *may* have soda. Eyes on me, people. This trip will be very instructive for all of you who—"

I noticed Hubert was watching Jean-Pierre instead of the teacher. I guess we all were.

I wrote a note and passed it along with my elbow.

Don't worry. I'll help with the new kid.

Hubert and I waited after class while Jean-Pierre collected a stack of textbooks from Mr. D. and stuffed them into a plastic shopping bag. Alyssa hovered at the door, trying, as usual, to barge in where she's not wanted.

Jean-Pierre saw us looking at the plastic bag.

"I was waiting to see what the other kids use," he said, shrugging. "I want to look like a New Yorker!"

"We all have backpacks." I turned around to show him.

"Billie would probably die without her backpack." Alyssa giggled, tugging on my strap.

I yanked away from her.

"See? Taking Billie's backpack would be like ripping the shell off a turtle."

Alyssa has been suspicious of my backpack ever since the day last fall when my puppy, Harry, came to school inside it. Thanks to my secret weapon, he was invisible at the time, but he wiggled enough to nearly give himself away. Now Alyssa pokes my pack whenever she can, just in case it will move. She won't give up the hope that she might uncover something to get me in trouble.

What if she knew the truth? I have to keep it hidden from my ever-curious little sister, so I carry it with me at all times. In my backpack is enough Vanishing Powder to make Alyssa disappear from my life.

3 • *Yo-Yo Boo-Boo*

On Tuesday, Hubert arrived at school armed with his own wooden yo-yo. Instead of waiting for me at the gate, he was across the yard with Jean-Pierre, practicing new moves. A few boys were sliding around on the frosty concrete, playing foot hockey with a tennis ball. But most of them were dangling yo-yos and hopelessly trying to do things that Jean-Pierre was doing with no effort at all.

"Hey, Hubert," I said, leaning against the brick wall next to the yo-yo seminar. "How's it going?"

"Oh, Hubert!" Josh and Victor warbled a duet. "Billie's here!" They made smooching sounds and shoved each other into the wall, like boys always do.

"Do you mind?" Hubert muttered to me. "I'm trying to concentrate."

"Allo, Billie!" Jean-Pierre flashed his crooked smile, his yo-yo spinning toward me in the same moment. I flinched, and he laughed, showing all his shiny teeth. "Come on, you want to try? I'll show you how."

I surprised myself by blushing.

"She doesn't have a yo-yo," said Hubert— kind of quickly, I thought.

"She can use mine!" said Jean-Pierre.

"I wouldn't do that," said Hubert. "She'll only knot the string or something."

All the boys laughed. Or, should I say, neighed? My face felt so hot my teeth were cold. I tried to grin like I was in on the joke.

With his right hand, Hubert dropped his yo-yo into the Sleeper position, rocking it forward and back on the end of the string. Then his left hand slapped his right hand, making the yo-yo jerk straight back to the top.

"Hey! Look! I did it!" Hubert's voice sang with pride. "I Spanked the Baby!"

"Wonderful, Hubert!" Jean-Pierre pronounced it *Ooo-bear.* He clapped Hubert's shoulder like a proud papa.

"Way to go, Hubert!" I cheered. But he was too busy high-fiving Jean-Pierre to notice me.

The school bell rang, so I had an excuse to leave. Hubert caught up with me outside homeroom.

"And you know what else?" he said. "This is the best day, already." He sounded so pleased with himself. "First, I did a Spank the Baby—after only three tries. He's a really good teacher, you know that? And plus, I asked him if I could call him J. P. instead of his real name, because it's sort of hard to say? And he likes it! He thinks it sounds like a cowboy. He wants me to tell the other guys, too."

Hubert had never said so many words together at one time.

"The other guys?"

"Yeah. You know. The guys."

"Hubert? Are you feeling okay? Should you maybe go down to the nurse? Because you are acting *strange!* Since when do you call Josh and Victor and David 'the guys'?"

"Oh, give me a break, Billie. You don't have to be the Queen of the World all the time. I have other friends, too, you know!"

He might have other friends, but as he stomped off I couldn't help thinking how I seemed to be losing my only best friend instead of making a new one.

On Wednesday, Alyssa came to school with her braids cut off. At first glance, I thought we had a new girl as well as the new boy. All her life, Alyssa has worn her hair in two long braids, like Rapunzel. And now here she was with most of it gone and an actual hairstyle—sleek but kind of flippy at the same time.

"Wow! Alyssa!" the girls buzzed around her. "You look great!"

The boys all noticed, too.

"Did you slip with the bread knife?" Victor sneered.

"Put the wrong wig on?" asked Josh.

"It's very *moderne*," said Jean-Pierre.

I didn't say anything because I didn't get why her haircut bothered me so much. *How dare you!* I wanted to shout. I got chills just looking at her. Suddenly she seemed way older than the rest of us. Well, me anyway. I didn't need a mirror to tell me that my freckles and my stringy hair the color of gravy and my stretched-out sweatshirt added up to no more than eleven. But Alyssa looked like a magazine model, or like someone we didn't know.

On our way to the library for Independent Study time on Thursday, Alyssa began to issue orders. Her new look automatically seemed to make her the leader. She tossed her flippy hair while she made her announcement.

"We're having a contest during I.S. Anyone with a yo-yo is eligible." It hadn't taken her long to realize that Jean-Pierre far outshone the other kids in the important skills of Skin the Cat (*Écorcher le Chat*) and Around the Corner (*Autour le Coin*). I could tell she already had dreams of throwing her arms around the official champion. But no one else seemed to care; they all dumped their books and pulled out their yo-yos, ready to begin as soon as my mother was out of the way.

Usually at this time I would have been with Hubert on the yellow chairs by the window. We liked to oversee the traffic on our corner of Sixth Avenue and Bleecker Street, making up stories about the people getting out of taxicabs. Hubert always invented the best names, like Dora Dipple, or Dr. von Tweezer. Sometimes we saw Mr. Belenky sneaking a cigarette between music classes.

But now Hubert was a yo-yo contestant, and Alyssa was making me sick, giggling and holding on to Jean-Pierre's arm. I couldn't bear to watch. I had research to do anyway, on Queen Eleanor of Aquitaine. I sat next to the biography shelf, trying to concentrate.

On her way into the Story Room to read to the waiting kindergarten, my mother sent me a secret wink. I pretended not to see. As soon as she left, there was a chorus of choked giggles from the study carrels and a brief argument about rules. I tried to ignore them, of course, but I couldn't help overhearing.

"I think J. P. should go last," said Alyssa. "Like, save the best for last."

"Why are you the judge, Alyssa?" David wanted to know.

"Because I thought of the contest."

"Not much of a contest if you already think J. P. is best."

"Fine. He can go first," she said. "To show you how to do the moves."

Finally they decided on alphabetical order. I couldn't resist watching. I found I could see pretty well through the middle bookshelf, between Helen Keller and Martin Luther King. Josh went first and totally flubbed. Hubert was next. He had his back to me, so I couldn't see the actual toss, but I heard everyone gasp like in a horror movie and then there was a nasty cracking that could only be something breaking. I stood up so fast I whacked my head on the bookshelf. Kids popped out of every cranny in the library.

Hubert's attempt to do an Over the Falls had sent his yo-yo through the glass of the Alumni Authors display case.

4 • Stone-Face

Hubert was staring at his hand as if it belonged to someone else. The other boys tromped on toes stepping back as fast as they could, as though Hubert were emitting poison rays. He stood still as a book, his cheeks white as paper.

"You're in for it now!" muttered Alyssa, instantly forgetting that it had all been her idea.

Oh, Hubert, I thought, coming around the stack to join the crowd. Oh, poor, dear Hubert. I wished I could sprinkle him with Vanishing Powder and let him disappear.

The door to the Story Room swung open

with a terrible force. I yanked Hubert out of his trance and pulled him over to stand next to me. My mother stalked in and scanned the library, soaking up the evidence.

Oh, Hubert, I thought again.

"Would anyone care to tell me what happened here?" When she's mad, my mother has a way of talking so quietly that you have to hold your breath to hear her. It's way worse than being yelled at.

No one spoke. No one moved even. I wondered how Jean-Pierre had managed to position himself beside the lectern with the giant dictionary. He looked as if he'd been working there all morning.

"No volunteers?" She crossed over to inspect the damage to the Alumni Authors display case. The glass was cracked from top to bottom but hadn't actually shattered out of its frame. The books were untouched.

Hubert's yo-yo lay on the carpet, like a murder weapon left at the scene. My mother's eyes swept back and forth.

"Billie?" she said, hardly moving her lips.

I nearly fainted. Oh, Mom, no! Don't do this to me!

"Give me the yo-yo, please."

No wonder I don't have any friends! I crossed the carpet, seeing only shuffling sneakers all around me.

I picked up Hubert's yo-yo and dropped it into my mother's hand like it was moldy cheese. I could never be a normal, popular girl with my mother at school every day! A person can't be herself when her mother's around.

"Can you tell me what happened?" she asked.

As if I'd snitch.

"No."

Several kids exhaled.

"I wasn't watching."

"Victor?" said my mother.

"Uh-uh," mumbled Victor. "I was tying my shoe."

That roused a weak snicker, but not from me. I felt like I could have heard Hubert's heart pounding, except that mine was too loud.

"Hubert?"

He trembled beside me and shook his head, not looking up.

"Fine," she snapped. "Since you're all unable to see properly at the moment, I'll take *all* the yo-yos for safekeeping until Monday."

She tapped the table. "Now." Five yo-yos were begrudgingly dropped by her drumming fingers, though I noticed Jean-Pierre's was not among them. Hubert's dangled from my mother's other hand.

"And this particular toy? This is now mine. Unless the owner wants to speak to me directly." She swept over us with another furious look. Alyssa was now skulking in the back row.

"Well," said my mother, "since you all seem to feel excess loyalty this morning, you have *all* assumed responsibility for this foolish accident—"

"But—" started Alyssa.

My mother ignored her. "—and you are *all* expected to appear tomorrow morning at seven-thirty for a detention. It will not interfere with the field trip. You will reshelve books and clean tables until class time."

A few kids had the nerve to groan. My mother raised an eyebrow in her special, chilling way, and the noise stopped.

"You are now dismissed."

"Oh, Hubert," I whispered as we filed up the stairs. "You must feel awful!"

"You better feel awful," moaned Alyssa, behind us.

"Awful?" He paused. "I guess, maybe. I'm sorry about the glass. But the thing is"—Hubert turned to me with a radiant grin—"I did a perfect Over the Falls! I really did it! Only the string slipped off my finger at the last second and went flying—

"Hey, J. P.!" Hubert called ahead, raising his voice in a way I had never heard before. "Did you see that? I did an Over the Falls!"

"You really are whack," I said.

"Yes, yes, I saw, Hubert!" J. P. smiled at Hubert as if he were a good puppy. "But tell me, please, this nasty woman is for real? We must clean her library?"

Hubert glanced at me, and a blush swept his cheeks.

I prayed for the floor to open up and swallow me. What chance would I ever have?

"Who?" Alyssa was eavesdropping as usual. "You mean Old Stone-Face Stoner? She's not just nasty. She's Billie's mother."

5 • *Detention*

I didn't even get my coat off before I was yelling at my mother. Jane ran for cover as soon as I opened my mouth. The smirk on Alyssa's face and Jean-Pierre's flustered apology had fueled me to a stomping rage by the time I got home.

"How do you think I feel when you single me out like that? Do you have any idea how completely humiliating it is to have my mother at school all day, sticking her nose in my life? Do you know what they call you?" I couldn't stop myself. I jumped off the cliff. "They call you Stone-Face Stoner! How do you like that?"

"Stone-Face?" She raised her eyebrows, but

she didn't fall apart the way I meant her to. She even almost smiled. "Stone-Face, huh?"

"How could you do that to me?" I whined, trying to get back on track. "How could you ask me to rat in front of everybody?"

"Billie, honey, I'm sorry." She reached out to pat my shoulder, but I shook her off.

"I wasn't thinking," she went on. "Someone spilled juice on the encyclopedia this morning, and then the copy machine was broken. It was the last straw having to deal with broken glass. Sixth-graders should know better. Sometimes your friends just get—"

"What friends? You think I have friends? Who wants to be friends with the librarian's daughter? Don't you get it? *I don't have any friends!*"

She gave me a long look and then spoke in her soft, let's-talk-this-over-I'll-be-your-friend voice. "Billie, aren't you being a little extreme?"

I gave her a long look back while my brain churned. It was all Alyssa's fault for calling the contest in the first place. Did it count as ratting if I ratted on her, since she's such a rat herself? I'd be protecting Hubert, and Alyssa deserved the blame more than he did. I hatched a devious plot.

"Okay," I said. "Maybe I have a couple of friends. But you can't try to make me rat on people that way. Because it backfires and they torment me. Especially if it was actually Alyssa's idea—" I gasped, as if it had slipped out by accident. "I mean—she made them—I mean—I don't really know, but the person who broke the glass was not—"

I fumbled into silence. The dirty deed was done. I'd planted the seed of blame on Alyssa, and Hubert was off the hook. Except that he'd have to buy himself a new yo-yo.

The next morning when I arrived to serve detention with the rest of the class, there was already a hill of backpacks just inside the door of the library. At home, I had purposely not been able to find my left boot so that I wouldn't show up alongside my mother. I added my pack to the pile and listened to our instructions.

She set us to work with an entire cart full of books to reshelve. I bet she had gone around randomly plucking books off the shelves to make more work for us. Even if everyone in the school had read a book yesterday, there wouldn't have been that many to be reshelved today.

The kids who arrived late for detention had to actually scrub tables. My mother had six buckets, six scrub brushes, six squirt bottles of some foul-smelling cleaning solution, and a stack of stretchy gloves like the ones doctors use. That's how toxic the cleaning chemical was.

I was delighted to see Alyssa show up at 7:45 and trip over my pack at the door, even though she kicked it when she realized whose it was. She had missed the cutoff time and was put straight to work scouring the tabletops, along with Victor, Renee, and Josh.

"This is *so* not fair!" she whined after one minute of forced labor. My mother ignored her, and I began to hum.

Alcott goes after Aiken. . . . Byars goes after Blume. . . .

"I don't see why we should have to do manual labor just because certain people"—Alyssa threw a menacing glare at Hubert, who was reshelving in Nonfiction—"are too clumsy to hold on to their yo-yos!"

"Shut up, Alyssa," warned Josh. The boys especially have a strict, anti-rat code.

"Well, I'm only saying—"

"Shut *up*, Alyssa," they hissed.

"If J. P. was here, I'll bet he'd agree with me," whined Alyssa.

Hey, where *was* J. P.?

"*Shut up*, Alyssa!"

"Alyssa," said my mother, sticking her head around her office door, "if you've finished with your table, I'd like to speak to you for a moment, please."

The library went as quiet as—well, a library. Two pink dots burned on Alyssa's cheeks. She shot me a look of blame as she peeled off her gloves and dropped them into a bucket. Oh, so what? I thought.

As the door to my mother's office closed, the door to the library opened. Jean-Pierre strolled in, his black hair blown wild by the January wind.

"Allo! *Bonjour!*" he greeted us.

"You're a little late, J. P.," grumbled Josh, pulling his gloves off. "We've done all the dirty work."

"I am sorry indeed," said J. P. with a cheeky smile. "I've been here only four days and already you miss me?"

Josh grunted, and the other kids laughed.

J. P. picked up a latex glove from the table. An idea immediately sparkled in his eyes.

"Watch this," he said. With one hand he bunched the wrist of his glove to his mouth and blew into it. With his other hand, he pulled out his should-have-been-confiscated yo-yo. As he held the inflated glove—

"It's an udder!" shrieked Megan.

—he flipped the yo-yo up and down a couple of times and then let go of the glove. It shot from his hand like an air-powered rocket and then *zap!* the yo-yo flew up to meet it and knock it off course, all in less than a second. It was a very deft trick.

"Wow! Hurrah! Score!" we all cheered in admiration. How did he do that—skip detention and have nobody mad? Everyone snatched at the gloves, and we soon had a game of multi-udder volleyball going on.

My mother's office door clicked open. We could hear the dreaded voice. All we needed was another detention! I grabbed a balloon from midair and pushed it out of sight into a bucket. Victor and Michele scrambled for the others. I shoved my fistful of extra gloves into the pockets of my jeans just as Alyssa clomped into the room.

Panic giggles filled my throat, but I swallowed hard at the look on Alyssa's face.

"You are a stinking, tattletale brat," she ranted at me. "Running off to tell Mommy when Baby Bertie gets in trouble!" She turned on Hubert, who was lurking behind Military History. "Well, you're in a lot more trouble now. I'm not taking the rap for a butterfinger loser like you. Stone-Face wants to see you next!" She crossed her arms across her chest and narrowed her eyes, brimming with satisfied vengeance.

Hubert pinched his lips together and headed to his doom. I grabbed his arm as he went past and whispered, "It's only my mother," but he pulled away.

"I'll come with you," said J. P. "It's only fair."

Hubert's grateful smile made my heart crack just a little. A stranger had thought of the right thing to say, and I hadn't. I felt horrible. I was his best friend, and I'd let him down. My whole rescue mission had failed because Alyssa had outratted me and probably told my mother every tiny detail.

When the boys came out, Hubert pushed right past me.

"Hubert," I pleaded. "Hubert, I'm sorry, I really am. Tell me what happened, please?" I tugged on his shirt all the way up the stairs, but he wouldn't say a word.

It wasn't until we got to homeroom, when Mr. Donaldson was going over the rules for the field trip, that I realized I must have left my backpack in the library.

6 · Field Trip

I tore down to the library, but my backpack wasn't on the floor where I'd left it.

"Mom!" I rushed to the counter. Had she stuck it in her office?

"Mom!" She was chatting with mothers from the Literary Committee.

"Library voice, please, Billie." She gave me her school smile.

"My backpack!" I screamed in a whisper. "Where's my backpack?"

"Oh, Billie!" I could tell from the way she rolled her eyes that she didn't have it. And I wasn't sticking around for a lecture on caring for my personal belongings.

Someone must have taken my backpack. I pretended for four seconds to think about who, but I already knew. Icy fingers of dread squeezed my neck as I climbed the stairs back to homeroom. If Alyssa had my backpack, she would waste no time looking inside. She'd find my makeup kit. And inside that kit was a film canister of what looked like shimmering face powder—

"There you are, Billie." Mr. Donaldson was waiting at the classroom door. "No luck? Don't worry, it'll turn up. We won't let you starve on the trip. You can share my lunch."

Oh, great, eat lunch with the teacher?

"Line up, people. Stay with your regular bus buddy, please. Look alive."

I pushed past everyone to get to Alyssa.

"Where is it?" I said.

"Do you see your precious backpack anywhere on my body?" She sneered.

"That's not exactly a denial, Alyssa." I didn't bother to keep my voice down. My hands were itching to shake her.

"Let's go, people. The bus is waiting. Billie, your buddy is up here."

No fair, no fair! I haven't had a chance to pummel Alyssa yet!

I dragged my feet to the front of the line.

My bus buddy is Michele. She's okay, kind of quiet. At least she wouldn't expect me to talk. We sat about halfway back. I let her have the window so I could try to spy on Alyssa from the aisle seat. I noticed Hubert had somehow traded in his bus buddy, David, for Jean-Pierre. And I noticed Alyssa and Megan were the last kids to get on the bus.

"Eeew, when do you think was the last time they cleaned this old rust machine?" Alyssa complained loudly.

Mr. Donaldson climbed aboard. He was holding my backpack.

"Billie Stoner? Is this what you were looking for?"

I couldn't believe it! I stumbled down the aisle and nearly snatched it from him.

"Next time, try looking under your own desk, Billie."

Wait a minute! It had not been under my desk, I know it hadn't. At least not while I was in the room. She must have gone back and stuck it there after I left. She is one prize sneak! I glared at Alyssa, but she was earnestly chipping away at her purple nail polish.

I returned to my seat and quickly unzipped the pack. Maybe I was wrong. Maybe it would all be there. It's not as though anything *looked* valuable. My lunch, my binder, my calculator, my library book.

No makeup bag. No orange-mesh-with-black-zipper-container-of-Vanishing-Powder makeup bag. She thought she was just taking a pretty cool bag. She didn't know what she really had. Oh, please let me get it back before she found out.

I stood up to go get it from her. The bus started to move. I sat down. What did I think she would do? Say, "Oh, silly me. Here it is," and hand it to me wrapped with a bow?

What should I do? What *could* I do? Tell Mr. Donaldson that my magic Vanishing Powder was missing? March up the aisle and punch her in the nose? Oh, sure. What a dumb mess this was. I so hated Alyssa.

I clenched and unclenched my fists, silently mouthing my tirade at her.

Michele looked at me sideways.

"Are you okay?"

"No," I blurted. "I'm crazy mad about something, and I don't know how to fix it." I could hear my own voice tremble.

"Oh," was all she said, turning back to the view outside the window.

Get a plan, I told myself, get a plan. As soon as we get there, I'm going to—And then I stopped, baffled. My brain was empty of all ideas. I couldn't figure out what to do.

I stood up again and sat down. My jean pockets were bunched up, stuffed with latex gloves from the library. I transferred them to my backpack. I took my jacket off, but then I felt cold and pulled it on again.

Alyssa turned around and sneaked a peak at me. I gave her the all-powerful Stoner Stone-Face Glare, and she dropped her eyes first. Hah. My brain started to work again.

By the time we got to the parking lot outside the Cloisters, I grabbed my chance.

I stepped between Alyssa and Megan. "Give

me back my makeup kit," I commanded. "Just hand it over now, and I won't expose you for the thief that you are."

"You've already got your moldy backpack," she said, "though why you'd want it, I'm sure I don't—"

"You know what I'm talking about, you snake," I said. I realized it was a mistake to confront her with Megan there. It just made her show off.

"Get out of my way." She tried to brush past me and continue up the path.

"Don't walk away from me." I stood my ground.

She pretended to trip and stomped on my foot.

"Ow! You rat!" I screamed, maybe a teeny bit louder than it hurt.

"It was an accident!" she cried as Mr. Donaldson strode over.

"Girls!" he huffed. "Your behavior is unacceptable."

"But—" I said.

"But—" she said.

"No *buts!*" He made us walk beside him while he started his lecture.

"The Cloisters is a museum that opened in 1938. It incorporates actual cloisters and chapels dating back to the twelfth century and imported here from Europe. A cloister is a place of seclusion within a convent or monastery. It might be a walkway or courtyard where one goes to reflect. As you will see, the ancient stone architecture and the tapestries and medieval artifacts inside give a real feeling of another time altogether."

We trooped up the wide steps to the entrance, with the stone ramparts looming above us. I pretended for a moment that we were knights returning to our castle after a crusade or a jousting tournament. There would be a goat roasting on the fire in the main hall and troubadours ready to tell us a tale. Except there weren't any Middle Ages in New York City and Alyssa was the only dragon around here deserving a lance through the heart.

I thought about pushing her down the icy

stairway and ripping open her bag. I could see her nose dripping with mud from my boots and her silver jacket soaked in slush. I saw her being carted to the dungeons by knights and left to hang by her wrists from chains in the ceiling, her face squidged up as she howled for mercy. I grinned for a couple of seconds before I realized I'd better come up with a more realistic plan.

Alyssa and I marched along, obediently following Mr. Donaldson, not looking at each other.

"Thief," I said without moving my lips.

She sneered. "Prove it."

"Oh, I will," I answered. "I promise I will."

7 • *The Cloisters*

*O*ur guide's name was Gerry. He was wearing a tie printed with coats-of-arms, and he didn't have much hair.

As soon as Gerry started talking, Mr. Donaldson forgot about us, and Alyssa slid away from his side like an eel.

"Look at the doorways in the Romanesque Hall," said Gerry as we stepped into the first gallery. "The finely carved details are worth close examination. They are lovely examples of the medieval belief that entering a Christian church was symbolic of passing through the gateway to heaven."

Well, here on earth, Alyssa was torturing me. Standing safely next to Megan, she took out a lip gloss and rolled it across her mouth in slow motion. I swear it was my own tube of Cherry Cola. Ohmigod, if she was already using my lip gloss, how long before she tried everything in the makeup kit? What if she pulled out the film canister right here? And yanked off the cap and spilled it all over?

"The heart of every monastery," Gerry went on, "was its cloister." He led us into a walkway lined with columns, surrounding a wintry garden full of dappled light. "And the centerpiece of every cloister was the fountain, or wellhead."

There was an old, stone, deluxe sort of birdbath in the middle of the garden, with no water

in sight. I guess it would be frozen anyway, this time of year.

I stood off to one side, shifting from foot to foot. My eyes were sore from watching Alyssa without blinking. I needed help. I let kids pass until Hubert and Jean-Pierre came up next to me.

"Hubert!" I whispered, catching the tail of his jacket.

"Aside from being a place of reflection and study," Gerry continued, "the cloister was the place where monks washed their clothing, using this communal fountain. They also washed themselves here, but probably only a few times during the year!"

"Eeew!" squealed Alyssa. "Information I do not need!"

"Hubert!" I said again.

"Huh?" He jumped a little, finally hearing me.

"My makeup bag is not in my backpack!"

"Huh? So?" His look was completely dense, as if I were speaking Portuguese. Jean-Pierre watched politely.

"I'm sure Alyssa took it." I emphasized every word.

Gerry was still talking, and Mr. Donaldson grimaced to shush us.

"Oh, Billie," said Hubert. "Give it a rest. You turn everything into a drama. You probably left it in your locker."

"But the Vanishing Powder from Jody is inside!" I had my mouth so close to his ear, his hair tickled my nose.

"Well, that's a dumb place to keep it," said Hubert.

"The cloister was also a passageway," Gerry explained, moving us along again, "and would have taken the monks to their daily meeting in a chapter house something like this one."

Now we gathered in a room with a fancy, arched ceiling and hard wooden benches lining the walls. Gerry told us to sit down, so I quickly squeezed in between Hubert and Jean-Pierre.

"This is where the monks would assemble to discuss the business of the day," said Gerry, "and listen to—"

"Hubert!" I poked him.

Mr. D. gave me another look. Hubert leaned away from me and made a big show of being fascinated with what Gerry was telling us. What could I do? I felt tears brimming up in my eyes.

I turned to my other side and found myself staring straight into Jean-Pierre's eyes! His eyelashes were about two inches long. My stomach rolled over and I looked away fast, swallowing the tears. Alyssa glared at me from the bench opposite. Hah, the least I could do was make her jealous. I looked back at Jean-Pierre and smiled. He totally smiled back.

"Any questions?" asked Gerry.

"Yeah," said Josh. "When's lunch?"

"Not yet, Josh," said Mr. Donaldson. "In fact, since it's too cold for a picnic, we'll be eating on the bus ride home."

"If you're hungry," said Gerry cheerfully, "here's something to think about. How do you like dried fish, kids?" He patted his nonhair, like he was being cool.

"Yuck!"

"That's what I thought you'd say! But if you were alive in the Middle Ages, instead of potato chips you'd be eating crunchy, scaly little fish wafers, straight from the barrel!"

"Gross!"

"All that salt might make you thirsty," continued Gerry. "But water was considered unfit as a beverage, so you would quench your thirst with ale or wine."

Jean-Pierre walked next to me on the way to the Gothic Chapel. My head was hot from trying to think of something to say. My neck was hot from not looking at him again. I felt like he was a magnet, and I was a pin, the way my whole self seemed to wobble in his direction. This was bananas! He was only a boy.

But, in the chapel, the only light came through tall, narrow, stained-glass windows. It was eerie and churchy and too dark to stand next to a boy. I moved off to a spot by myself and started to breathe again.

There were stone effigies of dead knights and ladies lying all over the place, as if all the pieces of a giant, granite chessboard were taking a nap. Victor started making ghoulie noises, but Mr. D. hushed him right up.

"This is probably Margaret of Gloucester," said Gerry, pointing to an effigy in the center of the chapel. "Effigies were made to represent and honor the dead, and to adorn their coffins. Margaret is presented in the highest fashion of her day. She is wearing a belt, as most ladies did, to carry her precious objects."

Like my backpack, I thought.

"She has a change purse, to carry coins for the needy. She has a sheathed knife—"

"Can you tell us about that, Gerry?" asked Mr. Donaldson.

"The knife was not for self-defense," said Gerry, "but more a symbol of her station in life. A lady who used a knife to cut her food was educated and elevated above the common folk. She also has a needle case, another sign of a protected, easy life. The engraved seam of her sleeve is a significant detail, too."

He pointed to a line carved into the statue's arm. "The more constricted a woman was by her clothing, the more important she was.

Real 'ladies' were literally stitched into their clothing."

Wow. Even in the Middle Ages, people cared about who was wearing what.

"Why doesn't she have any hands?" asked Sarah.

"The hands were likely damaged in transport," explained Gerry, "but they would probably have been carved in a position of prayer."

"Excuse me," I said. "Is it true that the punishment for stealing back then was having your hands cut off?"

"Hmm," said Gerry. As he started to answer I looked around for Alyssa to send her a knowing smirk. But Alyssa wasn't there. My heart lurched. Drat! I had gotten interested in the Middle Ages for five minutes and lost sight of Alyssa! She had probably sneaked out of the chapel and gone who knew where.

"Where's your twin?" I asked Megan a minute later, as casually as I could, with my whole self twitching.

"Bathroom," she whispered as we filed along to the Treasury on the lower level.

I stumbled down the stairs with the rest of the group, hearing nothing but wind roaring between my ears. I bumped smack into the glass door of the Treasury area, and that woke me up. Maybe she just has to pee, I told myself. Wait five minutes before you panic.

I tried to pay attention, but we were looking at case after case of silver goblets and gold chalices and buckles and brooches and clasps. Amazingly, I wished I were looking at Alyssa.

"We won't go into the gardens," said Gerry, "because in January there's nothing much to see except a few dry stems and gnarly twigs. Please come back in the spring and see the garden in full bloom! We grow many herbs and flowers used by medieval healers for making medicines and potions."

Potions? I was almost rocking with nerves. It was time to panic. Alyssa still hadn't come back to the group. I wondered how long before somebody noticed.

"Thank you, Gerry," said Mr. Donaldson. "You've been most informative. Let's collect our coats from the checkroom," he said to us, "and get back to the bus for lunch."

I held my breath.

"Mr. Donaldson?" said Megan. "Alyssa must be still in the bathroom."

"Well, go get her."

Megan was back quickly.

"She's not there," she said, shrugging. "She might have gone up the other stairs."

Mr. Donaldson sighed. "She'll be waiting in the lobby. Come on, people."

"Michele," I said, as calmly as I could, "you go ahead. I'm just going to check again for Alyssa. She, uh, wasn't feeling well." Michele joined the crowd pushing up the stairs, and I went down the hall to the ladies' room.

There were four cubicles in the bathroom. I leaned down to check underneath the first one and the second. No feet. Where had she gone? I pushed the door of the third stall, and it swung gently open.

Goose bumps raced down my arms. My neck burst into cold flames. My ears prickled. Spread out across the back of the toilet were the contents of my makeup bag: my lip gloss, my comb, my eye glitter. I reached out and picked up the open film canister that had held the Vanishing Powder. Every last speck was gone.

"Billie?"

I jumped nearly to the ceiling.

Alyssa's voice was right behind me. I spun around.

"Billie?"

You know how it says in mystery books "her blood ran cold"? Well, mine froze solid. The thing I'd been most afraid of when my backpack went missing had happened. Alyssa had used my Vanishing Powder. And now she was invisible.

8 • *Black Magic*

Alyssa?"

After all the times in my life I'd wished that Alyssa would vanish from the face of the planet, she chooses to do it in the bathroom at the Cloisters!

"I'm right here." Her voice was missing that bossy note. "Only, I—I—you know . . ."

"Yes, I do know, you stupid thief! How dare you! Ohmigod—you—you are—" I was so mad I was shaking. I scooped up the film canister and snapped on the rubber lid, trying to hold my shoulders still. I picked up the makeup kit from the floor and dumped everything into it. Then I slammed the kit into my pack.

Alyssa said nothing. I thought for a second she might have fainted, because Alyssa never says nothing. Then she made a weird, shuddery sound. It wasn't exactly a sob, but it came close. Like she was trying to stop herself from crying in front of me. I slowly turned around.

"I always knew you were hiding something," she croaked. "I don't know how you did it, but this could really get you in trouble, Billie Stoner. My parents could arrest you for this. My parents could put you behind bars in five seconds—"

"Wait a minute! Your parents are going to arrest me because *you* stole *my* backpack?"

"My parents are going to arrest you because

you're some kind of a creepy witch practicing black magic on innocent people."

That made me laugh out loud. As if I were smart enough to invent something this good! It was my friend Jody who was the witch—I mean, genius.

Then I felt a quiver of nerves. How *would* I explain this situation to Alyssa's parents? But I was determined not to show Alyssa I had even a moment's worry.

"And speaking of witches," I said, "take a look in the mirror. Oops, duh, it's blank! It's so typical that you are blaming someone else for your own stupid crime."

"And making someone disappear isn't a crime?"

"I didn't *make* you do anything, Alyssa. You *stole* from my backpack and then you *stole* from my makeup case and then you started to use my stuff! I am not even a speck responsible for your criminal act! Believe me, I'd rather be looking at your ugly face right now!"

I took a breath. I could hear my mother telling me that "an insult is the tool of a weak argument." I took another breath. Since I was right, I could lay off the insults and just make her—what? Make her say she's sorry? Make her reappear? Ohmigod! What was I supposed to do now? What was Mr. Donaldson going to say when he saw her? I mean, couldn't see her?

"Listen," I said. "We're supposed to be getting on a bus. . . ." What should I tell Mr. D.? Or should I not say anything? I felt trapped. I took a step toward the sink and crashed right into Alyssa.

"Hey! Watch out!" She grabbed me to steady herself, and my sleeve disappeared. My arm flickered, as if it might go next.

"Whoa!" she said, letting go instantly. "Did I do that?"

"Uh-huh."

"Do I have magical powers now?"

"No, you do not have magical powers! But while you're gone like this, anything you touch will disappear. So keep your hands to yourself."

She immediately gripped my arm again. It wavered and vanished.

"Let go, Alyssa! I just told you not—"

Without warning, the bathroom door flew open. Alyssa let go of my arm as Michele came in. She had nearly caught me shouting at an empty room.

"Billie, come on!" she said. "Mr. Donaldson is having a cow about you and Alyssa."

"I'll be right there, Michele. I have to, uh, use the facilities."

"Well, what have you been—"

Her ponytail disappeared. Suddenly her hair went dim and then was gone. Alyssa must have been holding on to it. Michele's face was intact, but she now looked like a hard-boiled egg with a face painted on.

Alyssa started to giggle. Michele jumped, and I laughed at the look on her face. But the laughter was coming from two directions. In an instant I knew I had to distract her.

"*Aaaeeeyy!* A spider! In your hair!" I shouted.

Michele clapped her hands to her head. "Get it off! Get it off!"

I flapped at her like I was helping, and she ran from the room with a howl. I fell against the wall and cracked up. I couldn't help it. And

Alyssa sounded like she was choking, she was laughing so hard. It was a couple of minutes before we caught our breath. I couldn't believe I was having fun with *Alyssa*!

"This could rock," she said. "This could really be a party. How long does it last?"

Hold on, I thought. She shouldn't be getting so pleased with herself.

"It depends," I said.

"On what?"

"On quite a few things."

"Like?"

I didn't answer.

"Like what, Billie? It just wears off, right? How long do I have?"

What should I say? I was thinking that maybe she deserved a little punishment. After all, she was still a dirty, rotten thief. Finally, I had some power over her.

"Clue number one," I said. "This powder does not wear off."

"What?"

"It does not wear—"

"I heard you the first time. But it's really creepy the way your eyes keep missing mine. You're looking sort of past me, like I'm not really here. It's distracting. So, anyway, if it doesn't wear off, what happens?"

"Hmm," I said. "I guess we'll just have to wait and find out, won't we?"

I wished I could see the face that went with her choking growl.

"You are totally whack, Billie Stoner. If you don't tell me right now, I'll—"

"You'll what? Sue me? Call the police? Report me to the Department of Witchcraft?"

"Oh, get lost!" she said, practically spitting.

That did it. I marched toward the door.

"Wait!"

I ignored her and pushed it open.

"Where are you going?"

"I'm getting lost."

9 · Hiding the Invisible Thief

I stomped into the hallway.

Alyssa was right behind me.

"Wait a minute!" she pleaded. "Please wait!"

I waited, but I didn't turn around.

"It really doesn't wear off?"

The tremble in her voice was more than a bit satisfying.

"It really doesn't."

"So what happens?"

There were heavy footsteps on the stairs, and Mr. Donaldson's feet came into view.

"Oh, no!" Alyssa's boots squeaked as she yanked open the bathroom door to hide herself. I didn't have time to remind her that she was invisible before Mr. Donaldson was looming over me. The bathroom door swung slowly closed.

"Billie, we have been waiting in the lobby for more than ten minutes. I'm fed up with your behavior today." Mr. D.'s jaw was clenched tight. "You are begging for a detention."

"But I found Alyssa."

"Well, where is she?"

"In the bathroom."

"What's going on here? This is not the time or the place—" He strode over to the door and pushed it open a couple of inches. He stuck his pointy nose right in the crack. "Alyssa Morgan? I want you out in this hallway by the time I count to five. One, two, three—"

"But—" she yelped.

"Four—"

"She can't come out!" I whispered at him. "She—she—she had an accident!"

He turned to stare at me, letting the door go.

"She's too embarrassed," I said.

"I knew I should have had a female staff member on this trip." Mr. Donaldson looked at his watch. "I'm not happy about this. Just get her onto the bus right away. The rest of the class are buying postcards in the gift shop, and the line to pay is ridiculous. We'll be out there as soon as I can drag them along."

"We need our jackets. It's freezing. Could you send Hubert with our jackets?"

"Right away."

He took the steps two at a time. I leaned against the wall, trying to steady myself. I could hear Mr. D.'s shoes echoing in the stairwell.

What now? Ohmigod, what now?

The bathroom door eased open.

"Is he gone?"

"Uh-huh."

"You are such a slimy toad!" she hissed. "You told him I peed my pants!"

"What the heck else was I supposed to say? I couldn't let him see you, because he can't see you!"

"You thought of the worst possible—"

Footsteps sounded again on the stairs.

"Quick, go in," I said. "That's probably Hubert. Oh, and take off your jeans."

Before she could say anything, I pulled the door shut and turned around to face Hubert. He was holding my jacket and Alyssa's puffy silver ski coat.

"Here," he said, shoving the bundle into my arms. His face was puckered into a glower. "What's going on?"

"I found Alyssa."

"So?"

"I found her, but she's invisible."

He put his hands over his face. "Oh, rats."

"Don't faint on me, Hubert. I need your help, I really do."

"I'm not in much of a mood to help you, Billie."

"Hubert, I said I was sorry. And I am. I'm really sorry you got in trouble with my mother. I truly thought I was avoiding that. Maybe it's not the best time for me to beg favors, but, please, pretty please, imagine the size of trouble Alyssa being invisible is going to get me in. Couldn't you help us? Please? Come inside."

"But it's the girls'!"

"Get over it," I said, nudging him ahead of me.

"If you think," started Alyssa, making Hubert

jump halfway to the ceiling. "If you think for half a second that I'm going to strip off my clothes—"

"It's a perfectly good idea," I said calmly.

"Perfectly stupid, you mean."

"If you take off your jeans, they'll reappear, and we can, you know, dangle them from your jacket and make it look like you. Or at least a scarecrow version of you."

"You are completely sick, Billie!"

You should talk, I thought.

"Can I say something?" said Hubert.

"You came up with the plan most guaranteed to humiliate me," complained Alyssa.

"Well, none of this would have happened if—"

"Can I say something?" said Hubert again.

"I refuse to walk around in my underwear, even if I'm invisible!"

"Maybe you and Hubert could switch jeans!" I cried. "Then yours would have real legs and—"

Hubert stomped his foot.

"Billie!" he said. "Stop! I am not taking off my jeans, and neither is Alyssa!"

"Way to go! Stand up like a man, Bertie," said Alyssa.

"All she has to do is get on the bus," said Hubert. "No one can see her anyway, jeans on or jeans off."

"The boy's a genius," said Alyssa.

"What about when Mr. D. counts heads?" I asked.

"Oh," said Hubert. "I forgot about that."

"Just give me my lousy jacket!" shouted Alyssa, snatching it out of my hand and making it vanish. "I'll meet you on the lousy bus!"

The door disappeared for a second as it whooshed open. Hubert and I were left gaping at each other.

10 • *The Haunted Bus Ride*

H ubert and I were galloping up the stairs before you could say *invisible*. But of course there was no sign of Alyssa.

"Pay attention, people. Line up, please." Mr. Donaldson was herding the sheep. I grabbed

Hubert's arm, and we ducked out the door to the parking lot.

The driver was leaning against the side of the bus, huddled into his uniform and puffing on a cigarette. The door to the bus was shut.

"Where do you think she is?" whispered Hubert.

"Not on the bus," I said, looking around for clues. "Oh, this just ticks me off so much! The rest of the kids are going to be here any second. What if this doesn't work? What if he thinks she ran away or something? What if he calls the cops? What about that, Hubert?"

"Maybe *we* should call the cops. I mean, seems like she really did steal your bag, huh?"

"Hubert, that's what I've been trying to tell you. You see why I've been acting whack? Do you get it now?"

"Jeez, yeah."

"Zzzzzsssssst!" One inch from my ear came a buzzing like a jumbo mosquito. I swung around and swatted Alyssa.

"Don't you ever do that again!" I snatched at her and found part of her jacket. The bus driver gave me a nervous look. I smiled at him.

"Could we get on the bus now, please? Medical reasons."

The driver flicked away his cigarette and pressed the hidden button to open the bus door. My fistful of Alyssa's clothing gave her no choice but to squeeze up the steps next to me. Mr. Donaldson and the other kids appeared under the arched entrance of the Cloisters.

"I'll just wait here for J. P.," said Hubert, lingering outside. "You guys go on ahead."

I tried not to feel disappointed that he was going off duty. He'd come through with the jackets, after all.

"Thanks," I said. "But there's only one of us, remember? From now on."

"From now on?" whispered Alyssa as I yanked her down the aisle.

"Until I decide otherwise," I said, trying to sound tough.

I took the window in the back row and made Alyssa drape her jacket over the top of the aisle so it would show.

Mr. D. must have taken Alyssa's predicament

seriously. "Everything okay back there, girls?" he asked, climbing aboard.

"Yes, sir!" I shouted.

"Yes, sir," squeaked Alyssa when I poked at her.

I guess Mr. D. had told the class to leave us alone, because no one bugged us or even sat near us. People were diving into their lunches, and we had the whole back row to ourselves. I noticed that Hubert was much closer to the front than he had been on the trip up.

As far as I was concerned, Alyssa should have been sitting quietly next to me, apologizing with every breath. But before the bus had gone ten blocks, I felt her move. I reached over and she was gone.

"Alyssa!" I whispered. "Come back here!"

No answer. Oh, she made a girl want to swear!

Then, after a moment, her annoying giggle came from across the aisle.

"Keep your hair on," she murmured. "I'm right here."

Suddenly a patch on the window steamed

up, like she was blowing on it. Then, magically, she drew a circle.

"Hey," I said. "Why isn't the window disappearing?"

"I'm using the tip of my sweater."

She made dots for eyes and stroked in a smiling mouth.

"Okay," I said. "Pretty cool. Now stop before someone sees." Silently, she added a tongue sticking out of the mouth.

"Ha-ha," I said. There was a rustle and a scrape as she stood up again.

"Sit down!" I said. I craned my neck over the seat in front.

Suddenly Josh was shouting. "Hey! What? Who took my—" He bounced out of his seat, making a noise like a scared dog.

Mr. D. hauled himself to his feet and glared at Josh.

"I had a bag of Gummi Worms on my lap," Josh explained. "And they just disappeared!"

"I guess you ate them even faster than usual," said Mr. Donaldson.

"No, I'm sure, I—"

"There's a field-trip rule, Josh," said Mr. Donaldson. "If you bring candy, you bring enough for everyone. Now sit down and put a lid on it."

I heard a bag crackle next to me. A Gummi Worm landed on my thigh.

"Maybe that'll sweeten you up!"

"Alyssa!"

But already there was a chorus of "Hey" and "Thanks, Josh!" and "Good aim!" as Gummi Worms flew through the air and landed in people's laps.

"And two for J. P.!" I heard Alyssa say before she retreated to the seat across the aisle.

Hubert stood up and waved his arms at me. "Billie!" he yelled, as if I had any control! In the confusion, miraculously, he was the only one who figured out what had happened. Then again, I suppose thinking a classmate had suddenly vanished and was now showering Gummi Worms in a bus on the West Side Highway is not the first thing a normal person would guess.

"Should I kill you now?" I asked. "Or do you want to kiss Jean-Pierre good-bye first?"

"Oh, lighten up!" she said, sneering. "You're about as much fun as a doorknob!"

Ouch. Was that true? I wondered. I'm fun, aren't I? Or is that why I don't have so many friends? Am I really Stone-Face Junior?

Alyssa was cackling so loudly that Mr. Donaldson was headed down the aisle. I jumped to my feet and flapped Alyssa's jacket in the air as a decoy.

"Sorry, sir!" I yelled, before he could come any nearer. "We'll be quiet, I promise."

"You sit down," I hissed at Alyssa. "Sit down, shut up, and count to a thousand."

I sat down, too, and prayed to wake up from this nightmare.

Finally, the bus turned onto Bleecker Street and came to a stop outside the school. The driver made a beeline for the deli across the street. Mr. Donaldson went up front to shepherd the class off. We waited in our seats until everyone else had left.

"All right, step on it now, girls," called Mr. D. "Do you want me to phone your mother, Alyssa?"

"No! No, thank you!"

"Don't worry about her," I said, inching forward along the aisle. "She was coming to my house anyway."

"I was not," muttered Alyssa, a step behind me.

"He doesn't have to know that," I muttered back.

"Fine," said Mr. Donaldson.

I was at the front of the bus now, hovering on the stair. How was Alyssa supposed to get off?

"I must say, Billie," continued Mr. D., "I do not applaud your method, but your behavior today was quite chivalrous. I'm proud of you for overcoming your differences and aiding a friend in need."

"Thanks, sir."

The driver crossed the street, coming back from the deli with a paper cup. He'd probably want his bus back.

"Come on, Alyssa," I said, in my cheeriest voice.

"Bye, then," said Mr. Donaldson.

I held my breath until the school doors

closed behind him. The bus driver was now in front of me, tapping his foot.

"Sorry to keep you waiting," I said. "I forgot my backpack." I fake-tripped a little on the step. He reached out his arm to save me and then took a step back to get out of the way. Alyssa scrambled past me onto the sidewalk. I smiled up at the driver.

"Thanks," I said.

"Have a nice day," he replied.

As if there was any chance of that.

11 • *Hot Air*

What do we do now?" asked Alyssa.

"It's a good thing we're back late from the trip," I said. "Most of the kids are gone, not to mention my mother."

"Hello? Billie! Remember me? What are you going to do about me?"

I tried to stare at her. I wanted to shoot her a killer look like my mother's.

"I'm over here, pinhead."

I was glaring in the wrong direction.

"Could you just tell me the spell or whatever to make me reappear?"

"It's not a spell, Alyssa."

"What is it, then? What happens?"

"What'll you give me to tell you?" Having an enemy was bringing out the worst in me. But, I admit, tormenting her came pretty easily. "I have information. You want information. Have you got any cash?"

"What? I'm supposed to pay you? Forget it, Billie," she said. "I'm going to follow you around until you fix me back. You told the teacher I'm coming to your place. So I'm coming to your place. And I'm staying till this is over."

"No way," I said. "My mother is at my place!"

"Well, we can't go to my place, Billie, because I won't be there! Even *my* mother would notice that!"

"I'm not going anywhere with you, Alyssa. I'm sick of you. And I feel like an idiot, talking to myself in the middle of the street. You stole my backpack, and you stole my makeup kit. I should have you arrested instead of talking to you. Plus, I'm freezing. So good-bye."

I turned to walk away. I took two steps and heard my name called. But it wasn't Alyssa.

"Allo, Billie!" Jean-Pierre had come around the corner behind us. He was wearing his adorable, crooked smile and no hat, as usual. How can a boy have such glossy, black curls while I have limp, brown straggles?

"Have you seen Hubert?" he asked. "I am waiting for Hubert."

"No," I said, "I have not seen Ooo-bear."

As cold as I was, I felt sweat under my arms. I knew Alyssa was still nearby, but I didn't know where, and it was giving me the heebie-jeebies.

"So," I said, flapping a dumb little wave, "see you around." I turned and tripped over Alyssa.

"Oof," she said.

"Oof," I quickly added, struggling not to fall over.

Jean-Pierre just smiled.

"Billie," he said quietly. "Don't go yet. I'm never alone with you, and I wanted to ask—"

Yikes!

"I was wondering—"

What? Wondering what? Oh, shoot, why did Alyssa have to be here?

"Would you maybe like to hang around? With me?"

"With you?" Was he asking me on a date?

"Oof!" I gasped again. "Don't!" Alyssa had punched my shoulder.

"Oh, please, do not be embarrassed," he said.

Embarrassed? I was flat out dying. Jean-Pierre was so not like a regular sixth-grader. Josh or David or Victor would never talk to a girl like this. They mumbled or teased. Jean-Pierre was—well, flirting! And Alyssa was listening!

"I know you are a bit shy," he went on.

"Hah!" squawked Alyssa.

"Ah!" I covered, squeaking like a mouse.

Jean-Pierre looked a little disconcerted, but he kept going. "I like that. Shy and funny, not so pushy as Alyssa."

My neck exploded in a rush of cold prickles. What was he saying? Oh, shut up, shut up, please!

"You are different," he continued.

"Ow, stop that!" Another punch. Like it was my fault he had seen the real her in only five days.

"Stop?" said Jean-Pierre.

I pulled myself together.

"I don't want to talk about anyone behind her back," I said just as Hubert came around the corner of the building.

"Hubert! Oh, Hubert, thank goodness you're here!"

"Allo, Hubert. We have been waiting for you."

Hubert rocked from left foot to right. He silently quizzed me, his eyes darting back and forth and his eyebrows pushed up, asking where Alyssa was.

"Hubert," I said, cocking my head in the direction of the last punch. "I'm going home, but I'll call you later, okay? I have to talk to you."

"I don't know, Billie." Hubert twisted his mouth the way he does when he's nervous. "I'm going to be kind of busy." He glanced at Jean-Pierre.

"Yes, call!" said Jean-Pierre. "I'll be there, too! I'm sleeping over tonight." He smiled. "It's good to have girls phone a pajama party, eh, Hubert?"

Hubert looked at me, and I realized we were both blushing.

"Party?" I said.

"Just us," said Hubert quickly.

Then, as I stood there wishing I was ten miles away, Jean-Pierre's hair faded and vanished. Alyssa was touching his hair! He clearly felt nothing, and his tan face kept grinning at us.

"Aaay!" yelped Hubert.

"Don't!" I screamed. It wasn't funny this time.

Alyssa let go. Jean-Pierre looked normal again, but completely confused.

"I have to go," I said, backing away. "I have to go home right now. I'm late." I didn't trust Alyssa for one more second. I wanted to run. I wanted to run till I fell down floppy like an old stuffed bear.

I did run, and pretty fast, too. Down Mac-Dougal Street to Houston, across at the light, and along Houston to Thompson Street.

"Billie! Wait up!" Alyssa's voice came from quite a ways behind me.

I ducked down Thompson and kept jogging as far as the M&O Grocery at Prince Street. The cold pinched my nose, and my breath came out in little frosty puffs.

Curiosity stopped me short. I could see my breath. I turned around. It was cold enough to see my breath. Could I see Alyssa's breath, too?

Lots of people were hurrying past on Prince Street, some with shopping bags, some with dogs. I stood there, panting from my run and squinting, trying to see if Alyssa's breath would announce her arrival.

"Thanks for waiting," she blurted sarcastically into my ear. I jerked toward the sound.

"Say that again."

"Say what?"

Wow! Sure enough. A tiny cloud of steam hovered in the air for a moment.

"Wow," I said. "I can see your breath. I didn't notice before because I wasn't looking in the right place, but—"

"Big fat deal," said Alyssa, shooting more

hot air into icy puffs. "What are you running away for, Billie? I told you, I'm going to follow you until you give me the cure. I'm coming to your place whether you like it or not."

1 2 • *Jane and Harry*

It took my dog, Harry, about three seconds to figure out that something was wrong. From the moment Harry heard my key in the lock, he started to jump as if he had springs on the bottom of his paws. I teased him with my mitten as we came in the door. *Boing, lick, boing, lick lick, boing.* Same greeting as every day.

But then he tilted his nose and his feet stopped dead. His little body was quivering slightly and he started to bark; quick, yappy barks, as if he'd spotted a cat and wanted to pounce.

"Uh-oh," I said. "Harry's too smart. And he's not too good at keeping secrets."

"What's bugging Harry?" called my mother

from the kitchen area. "Make him shush, will you?"

I picked him up and folded his face into the crook of my arm.

"Stay right behind me," I whispered to Alyssa. "And if you touch anything, I will tell Harry to chew off your hand!"

"Hi, Mom!" I said as I passed the kitchen and headed for the space I share with my sister, Jane. I held my breath. Alyssa was completely unreliable. I could feel her brewing behind me like a sandstorm.

"Hey! Where's my kiss?"

Aw, Mom! My mother kissed me and patted my hair.

"How was the trip, honeybun?"

I could hear Alyssa choke back a snicker. She was seeing a different side of Stone-Face Stoner, that's for sure.

"The bus was late coming back." I just wanted to get to my room.

"But how was the trip?" She was putting away plates from the dish rack, not listening too closely.

"Really interesting." If I said "really boring," I'd get a lecture about how an intelligent person is never bored. And what if I told her the truth—that my Evil Worst Enemy had stolen my Secret Invisibility Powder and was now stalking me on home territory? "Gosh, honey-bun, I've always loved your imagination. Why don't you write a story about it?" Oh, sure.

We live in a kind of house called a loft, which is like an apartment except it's mostly one big room with only a couple of half walls and doors. This is especially inconvenient when a person wants privacy or if a person has something to hide, which usually means the same thing.

Jane was on the bottom bunk, dressing her doll, Nonnie. The top bunk is mine.

"You share a room?" said Alyssa, at a normal volume.

Jane's eyebrows pulled together. This is what I mean by no privacy. If I was going to keep Alyssa hidden, I needed a miracle. Because Alyssa was too full of herself to be quiet. And Jane's wily brain sticks to secrets like Velcro. Harry squirmed out of my arms and started barking again.

"Oh, shut up!" said Alyssa.

Jane looked at me with an alert shine on her face. "You did another trick, didn't you, Billie? You vanished someone like you did with Harry."

Her eyes flitted right and left of me and settled where Harry was sniffing, at what must have been Alyssa's feet.

"Who's there?" Jane commanded in a stern voice. She groped forward like she was playing blindman's bluff. I heard Alyssa step back, her heel grinding a Playmobil doctor. Harry scampered away in alarm, whining a little.

I grabbed Jane's wrists and looked her straight in the eye. I was torn between admiring her cleverness and wincing from the horrible pliers of panic that pinched my skull whenever the Blabbermouth bumped into news.

"Jane," I said. "Janey-Jane-Jane. How about this: We're going to play a game. Let's pretend we have a visitor from, ah, the Forest of . . . Twinkenteenies, and she's a powerful sorcerer and—"

"And she's invisible!" cried Jane. Harry barked, almost like applause.

"Yeah. She's invisible. Her name is Toady-Breath and—"

That got me a kick behind the knee.

"And she's invisible because she's here on a Secret Adventure, and her very life will be threatened by Dark Powers if we reveal her whereabouts."

"And then what?"

"Oh, um, well, we better be nice to her, don't you think? We better serve her some fairy food. Will you go get her a snack?"

"Yes, yes! I'll get the food! I'll get Oreos! Fairy Frog Sorcerers love Oreos!"

She zoomed to the kitchen to find a snack. Harry bounded after her, nipping at her sneakers and barking joyful yaps.

"I'm not here to play some dumb fairy game with your kid sister, Billie. I'm really tired of all this. You've had your bad, little joke. Would you just do your stupid magic tricks or whatever? So I can reappear and go home?"

Go home? I suddenly saw a movie fast-forwarding in my imagination. Invisible Alyssa telling her mother why she wasn't there. Mother thinking she was hearing voices. Alyssa grabbing mother and shaking her to prove her story. Mother disappearing. Father tearing at his tufts of hair and calling the cops. Flock of cops arriving, dragging me off to jail wearing handcuffs.

"Go home?" I murmured.

Clearly, Alyssa could not go home in this condition. The full reality of our predicament washed over me. I was stuck with my invisible enemy.

13 • Cornered

What were you supposed to be doing after school today?" I asked Alyssa. "Won't your mother be wondering where you are?"

"I usually go home on the school bus. My mother gets home from the office around six."

"You just hang out alone?"

"Yeah, you know, I have a snack, watch TV,

tell her I'm doing homework. Oh!" She sounded dismayed for a second. "I'm supposed to check in or they dock my allowance. I should phone now. Where's your phone?"

"Jane!" I called. "Bring the phone, would you? I need to call somebody about homework."

"You should get a phone in your room," said Alyssa.

"No kidding," I said.

Jane came in with a plate of cookies and graham crackers in her hands and the remote telephone receiver tucked under her chin.

"Mom's pouring lemonade," she said as she unloaded. "I'll go get it. I told her three glasses, for a game." She winked and ran back to the kitchen.

I held the phone in the air. "You better do this fast. Jane'll be back in two minutes."

Alyssa snatched the phone away into thin air. A moment later it reappeared on the floor.

"You'll have to dial," she said. "I can't see the numbers while I'm holding the phone."

"Oh, cripes. What's the number?"

I dialed for her and handed it back.

"Hello? Extension number four-five-seven, please. Hello, Tina? This is Alyssa. Uh, fine, thanks. Is my mom there?"

"Who's Tina?" I whispered.

"My mother's secretary."

The seconds ticked by. I heard Jane giggle in the kitchen and ice rattling out of its tray.

"Oh, hi, Mom? I'm calling because I didn't go home on the bus today. I was invited to have a sleep-over."

"What!" I spluttered. "You were not!"

"By Billie Stoner," Alyssa continued, her voice as cool as cool.

I waved my hands where I thought her face must be, shaking my head back and forth. Alyssa sleep over at my house? No way!

"Uh-huh. Billie Stoner. Ms. Stoner's daughter. Well, I know I don't usually like . . . but . . . well, yeah, I know I told you she was . . ." Alyssa's voice dropped to a mumble.

Embarrassment hovered over us. I wondered what terrible things she'd said about me to her mother. Probably the same kind of things I'd said about her to mine.

"I'll borrow pajamas." Her voice was normal again. "So, it's okay?

"Oh, let me ask." Alyssa poked me, and my sweatshirt flickered for an instant. "When should I be picked up?"

"Now," I said, knowing it was hopeless.

"Get real. When? When is it going to wear off?"

"Tell her you'll call her,'" I whispered.

My heart sagged like a water balloon ready to pop. I was going to have to help her. I'd have to call Jody. I'd have to find all the ingredients for the potion. The talcum powder, the different fungi . . . The dog biscuits we have. I would need Hubert for the gum juice. Why did it have to be so complicated? I was going to have to—

"Mom? Can I call you again in the morning? We might do our homework."

Of course she didn't have to know I was going to help her. She deserved to suffer for as long as possible. . . .

"Yes, I promise. Yes, yes, I will. Okay, g'bye, Mom." The phone flew through the air and landed on Jane's bed.

"I did *not* invite you to stay here tonight," I said.

"Do you have any better ideas, you lame-brain?" Somehow Alyssa managed to sneer even without a face.

"You're the last person I want as a guest, Alyssa."

"Billie!" Jane was standing there, holding a teetering tray with three glasses. "It's Alyssa? The Frog Fairy is Alyssa? I thought you hated Alyssa!"

"Jane!"

"I'm not deaf, you brat, only invisible," said Alyssa.

"But how come she gets to be invisible, and I never do? I want to! When's my turn?"

"Oh, shut up!" yelled Alyssa.

"You shut up, Alyssa!" I said.

"I'm telling Mommy!" cried Jane.

I snatched the tray of drinks from her hands before we had a disaster. I put the tray on my desk and pulled Jane onto her bed, landing with the phone under my spine. Harry was on top of us in a second, yelping with delight.

"Janey," I whispered. "I know it doesn't seem fair, but being invisible isn't always a good thing. No one hugs you if they can't see you. People say rude things about you even if you're standing right there."

"I didn't mean to."

"I know, I know, I'm not mad at you. Actually, I'm mad at Alyssa for getting this way. But here's the thing. If Mom finds out, I'll be in so much trouble I'll be crying for a week."

"You will?"

She sounded intrigued instead of sympathetic. I tried to think fast. I knew it would be much safer to have Jane as a partner on this.

"If you can keep this secret," I promised, "I will give you such a big reward you won't believe it."

"What will you give me?"

"It'll be a surprise."

"Do I get the present tomorrow?"

"When tomorrow comes and we still have a secret, we'll talk about delivery."

I took a deep breath before I allowed myself

to say the next part out loud. "Plus, think of this: We get to have a sleep-over party, and Mom doesn't even know!"

"Mom doesn't even know what?" said my mother, suddenly arriving at the side of the bed.

14 • Help Wanted

We have a secret," said Jane.

"Oh?" said my mother.

"And I'm going to keep it a secret."

I began to exhale.

"For now, anyways," said Jane, squinting at me.

"Forever," I said, pinching her.

"I've ordered the pizza," said Mom. Our traditional Friday-night supper is pizza, delivered from Lombardi's, the oldest pizzeria in New York. "Why don't you get started on your weekend homework, Billie? Jane, you come along with me and wash those hands."

Let Jane alone with a hot secret and my mother at the same time?

"No!" I said. "Janey, stay here. I'll help you wash your hands in a minute."

She looked at me with total scorn. "I think I can wash my own hands," she said, prancing out of the room after my mother.

"Oh, shoofly," I swore.

"Billie," said Alyssa. "Why can't I just have a shower and scrub this stuff off?"

"It doesn't work that way. . . ." I let my voice trail off. She was getting closer, but I didn't want to tell her the truth just yet. I kind of liked keeping her in the dark. I'd call Hubert, right now while my mother was busy, and tell him to start chewing the gum.

I found the phone on Jane's bed.

"Who are you calling?" asked Alyssa.

"The Department of Missing Persons."

"Hello?" said Hubert.

"Hubert," I said.

"Oh, hi, Billie,"

"What are you calling Hubert for?" asked Alyssa. "To talk to J. P.?"

"Be quiet," I ordered, covering the mouthpiece. I pulled Jane's blanket over my head so maybe she couldn't hear everything.

"Hubert, I only have a second," I whispered. "It's an emergency."

"Is this about Alyssa?"

"Of course. Only I forget the names of those Chinese fungus things we had to get for Harry the last time this happened. Do you remember? Locust barf? Goat's hoof?"

"Goat's horn, I think. Why don't you call Jody?"

"I will—it's just weird to call her after all these months and say it's an emergency. Or she might have moved, or— I was just hoping maybe you'd remember. Plus, Hubert?"

"Uh-huh?"

I'd been asking him for a lot of favors recently, it suddenly seemed. No wonder he got sick of me sometimes and had other friends over.

"Hubert? I know you're probably a little tired of me right now, but I'm kind of in a panic. . . ." I heard my own voice wobble. "And I also need you to chew the gum. Lots of it."

"But, Billie, how am I—"

"I could never chew as much as you, especially with my mother around. I'll pay you back, however many packs you buy. Gum juice is an essential part of the Reappearing Potion, remember? Masticated chicle. And you are the master masticator."

"Don't bother with the flattery, Billie. Anyway, J. P. is here, and what am I supposed to tell—"

Someone poked me.

I pulled the blanket off my head, but no one was there. Meaning Alyssa.

"I gotta go. Just pretty please do it, Hubert? Okay? I'll call you tomorrow. Say hi to Jean-Pierre for me."

Click.

"You *did* call Jean-Pierre!" Alyssa's voice was right in my ear.

"Out of the way, Alyssa, I want to go check on Jane. I don't trust her to keep her mouth shut."

I hurried to the kitchen before Alyssa could protest. Jane was actually washing her hands and singing a song about a crow on the fence. It seemed like nothing to worry about, so far.

"Billie, set the table, will you please?" My mother had trapped me.

Jane dried her hands on her shirt and skipped back to the bedroom. I put out plates and glasses. I flung down the napkins and cutlery. Not my best job ever.

Back at the doorway of our room, I stopped short. The contents of my backpack were strewn across the floor.

"Hey!" I said.

"I know you're lying." Alyssa's voice was coming from near my dresser, in front of the mirror. "You're just trying to torture me."

"What?"

"She took your makeup bag," reported Jane. "I saw it disappear." She was trying on the latex gloves I'd brought home from the library detention. Harry gnawed on the corner of my binder.

"You probably have some kind of magic medicine right in this bag," muttered Alyssa. "So I'm just trying everything."

"Don't you think if I had the right stuff I'd be

throwing it at you?" I asked. "And good rid-
dance? I swear, Alyssa, there is no instant cure.
It's a highly scientific procedure." And let's just
pray it's strong enough to counteract such a big
dose of powder.

"Look!" said Jane. Her wiggling fingers did
not quite fill the gloves. "Monster hands!"

She was so pleased with herself I had to
laugh.

"Watch this," I said. "Jean-Pierre did this
cool trick today."

I inflated a glove for her, making the fingers
pop up and wave. Harry leaped for it. A second
glove from the pile disappeared as Alyssa took
it. We could hear her puffing away and the
scratchy sound when she tied the knot and then
poof! A balloon bounced out of nowhere and
boinked Jane on the forehead.

Jane teased Harry with it, wiggling the fingers in his face and pulling them away quickly
before his teeth could get a grip.

The door buzzer rang.

"That's the pizza guy," called my mother.
"Settle the squabble, please, girls!"

"Jeez, it was your own fault," muttered Alyssa. She grabbed another glove, but this time we heard the rubbery snap as she pulled it on.

"Doesn't this bring back fond memories of detention?" she asked. "The fashionable accessory for all occasions . . . and strong enough to withstand toxic chemicals!"

"Kids! Wash your hands! The pizza's here, ready and waiting."

"I'm starving!" complained Alyssa. She now seemed to be sitting on Jane's bed.

"Tough," I said. "You're having Oreo crumbs and lemonade. Prisoner's rations."

15 • UFO (Unseen Flight Operator)

I managed to sneak a slice of pizza for Alyssa while my mother poured glasses of cranberry juice. I rolled it up in my napkin, but it was leaking orange oil and was kind of disgusting. I balanced it on my thigh while I ate, until Harry discovered it and started to beg. Our table is in the living room, partway between the kitchen area and our bedroom. I was just inventing an excuse to go to my room when the refrigerator door opened.

It opened with a definite click and stayed open about two feet. Thank goodness I'm the one whose chair faces the kitchen! Mom faces me, so she couldn't see behind her, and Jane's view was blocked by the plant on the counter.

"Molly wiggled her tooth all morning," Jane was saying. "And then, when she leaned over the turtle tank—"

I wildly shook my head no, hoping that Alyssa was looking my way.

"Be still." Mom tsked, trying to listen to Jane.

"Maybe she bumped her lip or something on the edge—"

A container of yogurt floated out of the refrigerator and over to the counter.

"—and Molly's tooth popped right out and hit Plunker smack on the head—"

The cutlery drawer opened and a spoon flew into the air. It looked like we were haunted!

Alyssa was completely nuts, and this proved it. How long could my mother not notice a ghost in her kitchen? But it took me another second to realize what was really wrong with this picture.

"Oh, no!" I gasped.

Jane and my mother looked at me.

"Tell what happened next, Jane. I'm just going to get some more juice." I dropped the greasy pizza napkin on my chair seat and scurried into the kitchen.

"Ssst!" I snatched the spoon in midair.

"I'm hungry," whispered Alyssa, fighting me for the spoon. "I told you that."

"That's not supposed to happen!" I whispered back. "If you're holding something, it's supposed to be invisible, too!"

"So?"

"So, you didn't notice that you're performing magical acts of levitation while my mother is sitting right there? Something's wrong!"

Maybe the powder was wearing off! Could that happen? What if Alyssa suddenly reappeared? Or worse, what if *part* of Alyssa suddenly reappeared?

The cutlery drawer opened again, hitting my hip. Another spoon flew up and tapped me on the nose.

"Stop it, Alyssa!"

"Billie?" said my mother. "Is something wrong?"

"I had a spill," I called. "I'm cleaning it up. I'm scolding myself so you won't have to. In fact—" I suddenly realized the best way to get rid of my mother. "In fact, why don't you take the night off, Mom?" I poked my head through the doorway. "Jane and I will do the dishes before we watch our video."

"But I don't want to do—" Jane started.

"Why, thank you, Billie. That's a lovely offer." She gave me her warmest mommy smile. "You really are a wonderful kid, when you put your mind to it."

"Aren't I a wonderful kid, too?" whined Jane.

"Of course you are, honey. Now go help your sister." She got up from the table just as Harry slid the pizza bundle off my chair. I held my breath. "I've only got two more chapters in my book, so I'll be enjoying a cozy read in my room."

Harry could have his prize in peace.

I took a breath when Mom's door closed. "I have to call Jody right away," I announced. "Jane, you sponge off the table. And put the pizza box into the recycling bin," I added while I dialed Jody's number.

"But there's a piece left."

Jody's line was busy, so I hung up.

"Are you still hungry?" I asked Alyssa, opening the box on the counter.

"You bet," said Alyssa. The slice wobbled out of the box and hovered in space. I watched in astonishment as it shrank, bite by bite.

"It's magic!" said Jane. She clasped her hands together in front of her. "You're doing magic!"

"What if you start coming back in pieces?" I spoke my worry aloud. "What if your zazzy hairstyle starts floating around by itself? Talk about scary!"

"Very funny," said Alyssa. "Is there any more food?"

I put popcorn in the microwave and pushed start.

"You're not doing any work," complained Jane.

"I'm making dessert. Maybe Alyssa will do the dishes."

"Very funny," said Alyssa. "I already scrubbed your mother's tables this morning. Just because I'm wearing rubber gloves doesn't make me the maid."

"You're wearing the gloves? The gloves from detention?" It was like a beam of sunshine breaking through the ceiling of the loft! "It's the gloves! Oh, thank goodness! It's the gloves! Wait'll Jody hears about this!"

I dialed Jody's number again, and this time it rang.

"Hello?"

I remembered her mother's musical voice with relief. At least Jody hadn't moved.

"Oh, hello, Mrs. Greengard. This is Billie Stoner calling. May I please speak to Jody?"

"Why, certainly, dear." It sounded like somebody practicing scales on a flute. "One moment, please."

I could hear her calling for Jody, and then she came back on.

"Can she call you in a few minutes, dear? She seems to be in the middle of one of her little experiments."

"Could you please tell her it's very important? In fact, could you tell her it's an urgent emergency?"

"Ooh, that does sound exciting," said Mrs. Greengard, as if we were sharing an adventure.

I hung up as the drumming inside the microwave dwindled to hiccups. I dumped the popcorn into the yellow bowl.

"Watch this!" said Alyssa.

A piece of popcorn floated up from the bowl, double-somersaulted in the air, and then—*poof!*—disappeared. Alyssa chewed noisily to show us where it had gone.

Jane shrieked and clapped, jumping up and down.

Alyssa grabbed fistfuls of popcorn and

punched the air a few times before making them burst apart like fireworks and scatter onto the floor.

"That is pretty cool!" I had to admit. Suddenly I wished I were invisible, too. I wanted to do tricks and run the show. "Alyssa! How about I pretend to be making it happen! Like a wizard."

I put on a trance face and deepened my voice. "Lowly Popcorn!" I growled. "I Command you to come Hither unto the Teeth of Doom!" I snapped my jaws. A single kernel trembled forward and ended its life in my mouth. Another piece followed slowly.

"Make it go the other way," suggested Jane. She was rocking back and forth with excitement.

"Think you can catch, Alyssa?"

"I'll try."

I threw the kernel into the air, and it hit the ground.

"I missed. Do it again."

This time I tossed higher but softer. On its downward plunge, the popcorn vanished—*poof!*—into thin air. We all applauded, and I tried throwing another. And then another. We kept throwing and laughing, and the thought flitted through my head that I was having fun. With Alyssa.

The phone rang.

I grabbed it. "Jody?"

"No, dear. This is Patsy Morgan, Alyssa's mother."

16 • Phone Frenzy

O h," I choked. "Hello, Ms. Morgan."

"Who's on the phone?" called my mother.

"It's for me, Mom!" I shouted, my palm over the receiver.

"Alyssa!" I hissed. "Where are you? It's your mother!"

A flurry of popcorn fell to the ground.

"What do I do?" she whispered.

"Talk to her, I guess."

Alyssa took the receiver, and it hung in midair, dancing a little. I began praying that my mother's book was a really good one, with really long chapters.

"Hello? Oh, hi, Mom. Uh-huh. Uh-huh. Okay, that's fine. See you." The receiver clattered back into place.

"What did she want?" I asked.

"If she wanted you to know, I guess she would have told you."

The phone rang again. The receiver jumped into the air and dangled there by itself. Alyssa had answered our phone!

"Hello?" we heard her say.

"Who's on the phone?" called my mother.

"It's for me, Mom!" I shouted. "Who is it?" I asked Alyssa.

"Oh, hello, J. P." Alyssa practically whinnied. "No, this isn't Billie. Can you guess who it is?"

Jean-Pierre? Phoning me? Hubert's the only boy who'd ever called me before.

"Alyssa! Give me that!"

But she was too busy gurgling.

"You got it in one! I'm flattered! What do you want to talk to Billie about?"

"Alyssa! *Give* me the phone!"

"She's busy right now. She wants me to take a message."

"I do not! Let me speak to him!" I lunged in her direction, but she must have ducked sideways. The receiver dipped to the floor, and I grabbed air before crashing into the refrigerator.

"Teasing is not nice, Alyssa," said Jane, crossing her arms across her chest. "You should let Billie talk."

"Okay, I'll tell her." Alyssa giggled. The telephone was making an orbit around Jane.

The telephone's cradle sits on the counter. I reached over and clicked the button a couple of times.

"Oops!" said Alyssa. "Gotta go!" She slammed down the phone.

"What did he say?" I asked, hoping I was threatening the right corner of the room. "You better tell me every word he—"

"Kids!"

We froze. My mother was suddenly in the kitchen with us, making things very crowded. She took in the litter of popcorn kernels and Harry's trail of pizza slime on the floor.

"I thought the plan was to clean up the mess, not mess up the clean."

"We're sorry, Mommy," said Jane in her sweetest little voice.

"It was my fault," I said. "We got goofy. I'll finish the job, I promise."

"Well, okay," she said. "But you better get moving or it'll be too late to start a video. I've got one more chapter. Come in to say good night. And don't forget to brush your teeth."

My mother's bedroom door closed.

"Alyssa?" I whispered.

She must have slipped into the bathroom behind Jane. I was itching to shake Jean-Pierre's message out of her. Why did she have to be the one to answer? And what had he said? Well, at least I was the one he was actually calling, not her.

I was also the one who finished the dishes and swept the floor. Just as I put the broom away, Jane came bouncing out with her face still drippy.

"You should see!" she whispered. "Alyssa has the glove on while she's brushing! The toothbrush is dancing around by itself all over the room."

"Whose toothbrush is she using?" I asked.

"Yours."

Yuck! I went to the bathroom door. My turquoise toothbrush was rinsing itself under the faucet.

"This makes three things you've stolen from me today," I said. "Backpack, J. P.'s phone call, and toothbrush. Just so you know I'm keeping track."

"'Just so you know I'm keeping track,'" she echoed, in a nasty, piping whine.

"Don't you get tired of being a brat?" I asked her.

"Don't *you* get tired of being a brat?" she asked me back. "A bossy, no-fun brat?"

"Hey," I said, feeling slapped, almost. "We just were having fun, in case you hadn't noticed!"

The phone rang again. This time I got it myself.

"Hey, Billie!"

"Jody! Thank God! Oh, thank you for calling back!"

She was slightly out of breath. "Your line was busy. What's up?"

"Who's on the phone?" called my mother.

"It's for me, Mom!" I shouted back. "I've got trouble," I said to Jody, turning to check that Alyssa was still in the bathroom, out of earshot. "The worst trouble."

I explained the situation as quickly as I could, politely not using the word *thief,* and not even getting to the part about the gloves before Jody interrupted me.

"Oh, this is good," she said. "This is very good."

"Maybe you didn't understand," I said. "From over here, it's not good at all!"

"What I mean is, from a scientific point of view, this is excellent timing. I've been testing a new recipe, and I was just thinking how I was ready for a human subject. I've replaced the fungi with dog food and mushroom soup for quicker action. This is a perfect test opportunity. Can you come up to my place now?"

I thought for half a second about telling my mother I had to go uptown alone in the wintry

dark of night to assemble the Miraculous Anti-
dote to my Invisibility Powder.

"How about tomorrow morning?" I suggested.

"Well, the only thing is, my mother is having
her gruesome gang of friends here for morning
coffee. It's her turn to be hostess. They get together every month to play Spite and Malice,
which is a card game, believe it or not, and no
way on the planet am I going to hang around
here to watch my mother cheating at cards
while the ladies swoon over her macaroons,
which she gets from Goldberg's Bakery anyway."

Sounds like Alyssa, I thought.

"So what you're saying is . . . ?"

"So what I'm saying is, I'll be happy to help.
I'm going to take notes, if you don't mind, and
I'll supply the ingredients. I've got everything—
oh, except for the gum! I still have braces, like
forever, so I can't do the gum. Is that cute little
Hubert available?"

"Yes," I said, hoping it was true.

"Okay, I'll bring the rest and meet you
somewhere far from the crone-fest in my living
room. Where and when?"

It was way too cold to meet on a corner. We finally agreed on the Barnes & Noble at Eighty-second and Broadway, in the kids' section, at noon.

I hung up feeling queasy. It was a good thing I couldn't see Alyssa, because I wouldn't have been able to look her straight in the eye. Jody's mention of dog food really had me worried.

17 • *In the Dark*

Jane fell asleep on the floor, snuggled in her sleeping bag. Above me, the bunk creaked and then creaked again as Alyssa turned over. So, she was still awake, too. Here we are, I thought—fire-breathing enemies sharing a bunk bed. In a movie it would be funny. Only it was real life, and never in a million years would I have invited Alyssa to sleep over. In fact, I was supposed to be ignoring her, according to my New Year's resolution. But here she was, practically moving in with me! This is *not* what I meant when I vowed to make new friends! Jean-Pierre, on the other hand . . .

"Alyssa? Are you asleep?"

"No."

"Why did Jean-Pierre call?"

There was a thump from above. I wondered if the blankets were invisible. Are things still invisible in the dark? The streetlight outside cast a glowing moon on my ceiling, but otherwise, the room was dim.

"What did he say?" I asked again.

"He wouldn't tell me," she said at last. "He said it was private."

"Private? He said private?"

"Are you—you know—are you a couple with him?"

"Give me a break, Alyssa. He's been in the school for five days!"

"Yeah. But he asked you out, right? Today, before Hubert showed up."

"Not really." I wasn't sure how much she'd overheard. "He's just got a French way of making friends, maybe."

"Well, I'd go out with him in five seconds," she said.

"Go where?" I asked, pretending to be dense.

"Oh, don't be dopey. If you're going out, it just means you talk more on the phone and stuff. Doesn't he have the cutest accent?"

"Uh-huh."

Maybe she wanted me to talk some more, but I didn't know what to say. I didn't feel so mad by now, just tired. Tired of having her around. Tired of the whole stupid situation. You'd think if someone was invisible, you'd see less of them, but Alyssa was with me more than ever.

An ambulance siren started in the distance, coming closer and closer down Broadway, turning into a wail. Hearing a siren at night always sort of scares me. It sounds so full of panic, and there's no way to know if it gets wherever it's going on time. I held my breath as it roared past our building and out of hearing.

"Did you like it when you were invisible?" Alyssa suddenly asked. It sounded like she was leaning over the side of the bunk. "Was it fun?"

"Yeah, it really was, at the beginning. First

thing I did was scare the underpants off Hubert. I sneaked up on him in the cafeteria, and he nearly choked on a tortellini."

Alyssa giggled.

"Then I skipped out of school and went for a walk around the neighborhood. It was totally fun; I even went on a movie set. I went to Dean & Deluca and saw a pickpocket. Then, when I got back to school, I—" I stopped short.

I'd almost accidentally told her the highlight of being invisible, which had been getting revenge on Alyssa. She'd stolen Hubert's topic of China for the fifth-grade class project, so I ruined her final presentation by sprinkling just enough powder over her notes to make them vanish. She got up to talk, and she had nothing to read. She couldn't rely on her memory because she'd copied the work in the first place without paying attention. I'll never forget the look on her face when she flubbed in front of everybody.

Now that I was thinking about it, it sounded pretty cruel. I mean, she was my enemy and everything, but maybe humiliation in public was going too far.

"Yeah? Then what?"

"Well, nothing, actually. I came back to school. Being invisible didn't really fit in with my life, you know? It's fun for a while, but it's kind of inconvenient. There's lots of stuff you can't do."

"So then what? How did you reappear? Really? Can I get normal tomorrow?"

Now that she was asking in a nice, ordinary way, I felt like I should tell her the truth. I mean, of course she'd want to know. I'd want to know if I were her.

"You said before, it was a scientific procedure," said Alyssa. Her voice went low. "Does it hurt?"

She was scared.

"It doesn't hurt," I said. "It's sort of a—a potion. It's a bit disgusting, maybe, but it doesn't hurt."

"Oh, great. I have to drink some nasty concoction?"

I think I was afraid to tell her.

"Er, no, you don't have to drink it."

"Well? What then?"

I decided maybe I'd better not say after all. She'd go bananas.

"It doesn't hurt, Alyssa, I promise you that. Jody will tell you everything tomorrow, okay? It'll all be over tomorrow."

"How am I supposed to sleep, not knowing?" she said. "Besides, it's weird being in your house. We're not exactly friends or anything, but I'm lying in *your* bed, depending on *you* for help."

And what if the new recipe didn't work? What if it turned out I couldn't help?

"Plus," said Alyssa, "I don't have sleep-overs very often."

"You're kidding. What about Megan?"

"I don't like Megan's house. Her brothers are thugs."

"Why doesn't she stay at your place, then?"

She didn't answer for a while.

"Oh, well, my parents . . ." she started, and then faded away. She was quiet so long this time, I was sure she'd gone to sleep. I lay there thinking about how to get an extra breakfast tomorrow.

But then, "You know what's strange?" she

said. Her voice was getting smaller and smaller, as if she didn't really want to be talking, but it was leaking out anyway.

"I sometimes get this feeling, when I'm at home with my parents, that I'm not really there."

"What do you mean?"

"They ignore me most of the time. I try to be funny and say clever things so they'll at least turn their heads in my direction. But they just keep on talking and talking to each other."

The bed above me creaked again. Alyssa's voice came more clearly. "They're in the same law firm, so they're together all day, too. They come home chuckling about some woman at the office or complaining about the waiter at lunch, and I sit there thinking I must be invisible."

Her voice dropped to a whisper. "And now I am. Invisible. Isn't that weird?"

"Yeah." And sad, I was thinking. I never knew Alyssa was covering feelings like that. You'd never guess from her regular self.

"It's the opposite at my house," I said. "I've got a Leech Mother. Talk about a Friend Repellent! Did you ever think about that? She hears what we're saying before we even think it. Plus, she's at school all day and knows what happens there, too. I feel all clogged up from having her watching me every minute."

"Well, I was listening to your mother go smoochy on you, calling you 'honeybun' and everything, and I was going to say something, you know, rude. But at least she's thinking about you. A pet name is not *so* bad. It's usually a sign of affection."

"That's true."

"Can't you just tell her to back off a little?"

"I try, but she gets insulted."

"Which do you think is worse?" asked Alyssa. "Being loved too much or not enough?"

"They're about the same, I guess." I didn't really think so, though. I knew however annoying my mother was, I'd rather have her there than not there.

I felt bad for Alyssa. She was sort of alone. Maybe being invisible was starting to take the crusty shell off her. If only she would keep it off.

I fell asleep thinking that if I never had to see her again, maybe we could be friends.

18 · Flustered

Alyssa and I waited for Hubert on the uptown platform of the R train. He lives near the Canal Street Station and I live half a block from the Prince Street station, so if we stand in the right spot, it's easy to meet on the train.

My mother had taken Jane to Katie's birthday party. Harry was safe with Sam, our totally cool dog-walker. And that was it for the plus side. I felt almost dizzy from thinking about the minus side.

Had Hubert chewed enough gum? Would the new recipe work? Would we be finished in time to meet Mom at my father's place uptown like I was supposed to?

"I wish this was all over," said Alyssa.

"So do I."

The train chugged into the station. When

the doors slid open, Hubert was blowing a bubble and waving from inside. And Jean-Pierre was standing right beside him.

Oh, no! How could we do what we had to do with Jean-Pierre around?

"Oh, goody," whispered Alyssa as we stepped onto the subway. "Your boyfriend is here. This'll be fun!"

"He's not my boyfriend, Alyssa," I reminded her through gritted teeth. I didn't want us to fight this morning, but she seemed to have her shell at least partway back on.

"Hi, guys," I said, glaring at Hubert as the train started. I grabbed the same pole they were holding. Alyssa must have, too. The whole pole vanished beneath my mittens.

"Let go!" I shouted. "Sit down!" The pole reappeared.

"Billie, I can't take this," said Hubert.

"What happened?" asked J. P.

"The lights play tricks in the tunnel," I answered, looking around for a clue to where Alyssa had gone.

"The lights?" said Jean-Pierre.

The seats were about half full. We were the only ones standing up. She might be anywhere in the car. I could almost hear the bomb ticking.

"Billie?" said Hubert.

"Huh?"

"I said, are you okay?"

"Me? Oh, sure. Surely, surely, indeed." My mouth was talking without my brain. I squeezed my eyes closed and opened them again to help me focus.

"How was the sleep-over?" I asked. "Did you guys stay up late?"

"Not too late," said Jean-Pierre.

"Felt like all night," said Hubert at the same time.

What did that mean?

People pushed in through the doors at the next stop. I noticed the number of empty seats was shrinking.

"We had 'boy talk,'" said Jean-Pierre, grinning at me.

Hubert flinched. What was going on here? I wondered.

"Hey, Bertie," said Alyssa out of nowhere on my left. "What color are J. P.'s pajamas?"

Jean-Pierre's head snapped up, and he stared at me. Hubert's eyes widened. I took a firm step to one side, intending to crush every bone in Alyssa's toes. Why couldn't she just be quiet for one more hour?

"My pajamas?" asked Jean-Pierre.

"Ha-ha, no, no," I said, squeaking my voice to sound more like Alyssa. "I was just—er—ha. That didn't come out the right way. What I meant was, it's a bit funny, you know? J. P.'s pj's. That's what we call them in English: pj's."

Alyssa giggled, and I swung my backpack into what I hoped was her rib cage.

"It could be a nonsense rhyme," I babbled.

"J. P.'s pj's,
He could wear them many ways,
Back to front or upside down,
In the sky or underground!"

What was I doing, reciting poetry about a boy's pajamas on a subway? The obvious answer was that Alyssa had finally managed to drive me insane.

"Billie," said Jean-Pierre, "you—you are— *extraordinaire!*"

Hubert looked as sick as I felt. The train squealed as we pulled into Forty-second Street.

"Don't we change here?" asked Hubert.

"Ohmigod!" I rushed for the door. "Come on! It's our stop, everybody!" I looked around frantically as I jumped onto the platform. People shoved past on both sides.

"Billie?" said Jean-Pierre, probably wondering why I was blocking the exit.

"I'm right here, honeybun," said Alyssa, next to me.

"Guys, go on ahead." I pretended to pause on the stairs to tie my sneaker. "I'll meet you on the uptown 1/9 platform."

As soon as they were a few steps ahead, I began to mutter. "Listen to me, Alyssa. Can you hear me? Alyssa?"

"Yeah, yeah."

"I'm helping you, Alyssa."

I noticed a woman yank her child away from me, and I realized how strange I must seem, babbling to no one. But I had to set things straight.

"Are you listening, Alyssa? I want to help you, I really do."

"Whatever," she said, like I was boring her.

"Alyssa? If we both make an effort—"

"You just make an effort to fix me, Billie!"

Oh, she was so annoying!

"Fine," I said. I'd given her a fair chance to be friends, and she hadn't taken it. I wished she had, but she hadn't.

"Just be quiet," I said, "since that's the way you want it! Do whatever I say, or I swear I'll leave you like this forever!"

I didn't give her a chance to make another rude comment. I ran to catch up with the boys, pretty sure she'd follow, at least for five minutes.

19 • On the Spot

Alyssa tripped on my heels getting on the number 1 train, so I knew she had followed us on board. I sat down. There was only one spot beside me, and Jean-Pierre took it. Hubert stood, wedged between a man with four shopping bags and a teenager with his Walkman turned up so loud we all could have been dancing. I couldn't tell where Alyssa was.

"Are you here?" I said aloud.

"I'm here," said Jean-Pierre, nudging me. "Why didn't you call me back at Hubert's house last night? Did Alyssa tell you my message?"

"No. She said—"

I got punched on the shoulder. "Ow!" I rubbed the spot. "I told you not to do that!" I guess Alyssa was pretty close by.

"What?" said Jean-Pierre.

"Never mind," I said. "What were you—" I stopped. What if he did have a crush on me? What if he said it out loud? What if Alyssa heard? I suddenly felt very hot under my jacket.

"It's about Hubert." Jean-Pierre leaned in close. I caught my breath. I could smell his shampoo. Lemon.

"I think I made a mistake last night," he was saying. "I should have noticed before, but I didn't. You probably think I'm an idiot. . . ." He paused.

"What are you talking about?" I asked. *Idiot* was not the word I had for Jean-Pierre.

"Until last night, I didn't realize—I guess I should have—that you were Hubert's, er, you know, that you and he are sort of hooked up," he said. "You should have told me. I looked so— I mean, if you'd told me, I wouldn't feel so stupid, asking you myself."

"What?" I said.

"What?" gasped Alyssa.

"You and Hubert," said Jean-Pierre.

"He *said* that?" I asked, quickly making certain that Hubert couldn't hear.

"Well, not exactly," said Jean-Pierre, "but I could tell from the color of his face when I told him that I—well—that I—"

He wasn't looking at me anymore. He was fiddling with the silver button on his denim jacket. I could practically feel Alyssa's breath in my face, so I knew she must have been eavesdropping really close.

"Oh, Hubert always turns red," I said. "It doesn't mean anything."

"But since then, he hasn't spoken to me," said Jean-Pierre. He stared down at his boots.

"Poor guy," said Alyssa.

Jean-Pierre looked up again. "Who's the poor guy? Me or him? I didn't mean to mess up. He was my best new buddy. You and me, we can still be friends, right? And you'll tell him that I made a mistake?"

My face was so burning hot I thought I might explode.

"Can we not talk about this anymore?" It

was the most embarrassing minute of my entire life, I swear. Hubert *liked* me? Jean-Pierre *liked* me? Oh, why did Alyssa have to be there, listening to every word?

"Hey, Billie," called Hubert. He hadn't heard, thank goodness! He squeezed past the guy with the headphones and stood over us with his knees knocking mine.

Hubert *liked* me? No way. J. P. must have made a mistake. Hubert was my best friend. He didn't *like* me!

"Which stop is it?" Hubert blew an enormous bubble.

"Seventy-ninth Street. Two more. And don't dry out the gum," I reminded him. "It's supposed to be juicy."

Hubert opened the pocket of his fleece vest, showing me the bulge of a Ziploc plastic bag, only half full of dripping gum blobs.

"We need way more," I said. "Keep chewing."

"I'm doing the best I can," he grumbled.

Maybe Hubert just didn't want J. P. to like me because he thought he'd lose his new friend. Or maybe he wanted to protect me from being embarrassed. Or maybe J. P. had it all wrong because he didn't know Hubert like I did. Or maybe—oh, make my brain stop! I couldn't think about this on the subway!

"Where are we going anyway?" asked Jean-Pierre as the train left Seventy-second Street.

"We're going to a bookstore to do research." Well, it was sort of true. I stood up. Ours was the next stop.

"Research?"

"For our project," said Hubert, catching on.

"Our science project," I said. "For extra credit."

"What is the topic?" asked Jean-Pierre.

"It's a study of the—ah—" Hubert was stumped.

"Particle Evaporation," I said. "The Dynamics of Disappearing Particles and Other Phenomenons of Altering the Boundaries of Perception."

Alyssa snorted. I leaned on her.

The boys stared at me in bewilderment.

"Right, Hubert?"

"Uh, yeah, uh-huh."

I heard a quiet *snap* and a shuffle close by.

It sounded exactly as though Alyssa was putting on the latex gloves.

"Don't you dare," I whispered.

"Lighten up," she whispered back. "It's research."

20 • Jody's New Recipe

All the way to Barnes & Noble, I tried to walk tall, taking deep breaths. First things first. We had to fix Alyssa before she churned up more trouble.

"Hubert," I said in a hurried whisper. "Go to the science section. Write down titles and stuff, just to keep J. P. busy. We'll meet you by the doors in twenty minutes. And keep chewing!"

Alyssa trailed after me up the escalator.

"I don't like this, Billie," she said, barely lowering her voice. "Does all that disgusting gum that Hubert is chewing have anything to do with me? And what about J. P. asking you out? You said—"

I buried my face in my bag. One thing I was definitely not discussing with Alyssa was boys. "Alyssa, in five minutes we're meeting Jody. She's the Powder inventor. She'll make everything normal so you can go home. Until then, keep your hands in your pockets and shut up. We're in a bookstore. It's practically a library!"

In the junior section, they have a little story-time stage draped with baby-blue curtains, as if Mother Goose is going to turn up any minute to put on a show.

Jody was sitting cross-legged on her jacket in the middle of the platform, reading *Curious George Gets a Job.* I hadn't seen her for months, but she looked just the same, like an overgrown elf with big ears and floppy hair and braces and an odd, orange shirt with RODNEY embroidered on the pocket. She comes across as way younger than sixteen, but she doesn't seem to care.

"Hey!" she said, looking up as we arrived. "Don't you love Curious George? I always loved him. I wanted to marry the Man in the Yellow Hat and live with Curious George and have escapades. *Escapades* is such a good word, don't you think? I thought it would be much more exciting than living with my parents."

"*This* is the person who's supposed to save my life?" said Alyssa. "I should have known. With Billie running the show, the most I could expect was a freak."

"Alyssa! Shh! Jody is the smartest person you'll ever meet."

Jody's eyes locked with mine and then danced over to where Alyssa's voice had come from. I checked behind me quickly, making sure no shoppers were nearby.

"Hmm," said Jody. "A nervous subject, eh? I guess we'd better get on with it. We don't want this situation to linger any longer than necessary! Did you bring the gum, Billie?"

"Hubert has it. He's meeting us downstairs."

Jody pulled on a fuzzy plaid jacket, making her look like an elfin lumberjack. She herded us toward the escalators.

"I've checked out the ladies' room here, but I don't think it's going to work. The sinks are tiny, and the toilets would clog up in a second. We really do need a bathtub. Got any ideas?"

She didn't wait for an answer.

"Full immersion is always most effective. The new recipe has some real benefits, like being able to shop at Fairway for Power Puppy Pork Chunks any day of the week instead of beetling down to Chinatown for fungi."

"Wait a second!" interrupted Alyssa.

We stepped off the escalator and wove our way through the tables toward the door. All the holiday books were on sale, and lots of readers were browsing.

"Dog food seems to work faster," Jody continued, "but she still has to soak for at least—"

"I said, stop right there!" Alyssa burst out.

I'd been dreading this moment.

"Let me get this straight. Did you say 'soak in dog food'?"

I shook my head at Jody, signaling her to proceed carefully, or maybe even outright lie, but she was focused on the space where Alyssa seemed to be. A man with earmuffs was watching us. I hoped he couldn't hear properly.

"It's a mixture of dog food and mushroom

soup," Jody explained, trying to convince us both, I guess. "It's freeze-dried in a sort of primitive manner, in waxed-paper pouches. My mother found a few lumps in the freezer last week, and I told her they were rum truffles from the Festivals of Other Cultures class at school. She wanted to know which culture so we'd never go there on vacation.

"But the freezing reduces the odor and makes the substance much easier to work with. There's really nothing to be worried—"

A whole stack of books flew to the floor with a tremendous *thump*. Apparently, Alyssa was wearing the gloves!

"This was all part of your plan from the beginning, wasn't it, Billie Stoner?" Alyssa hissed. "You only pretended to have fun and do tricks and everything, just to lure me into the hands of some weirdo science cult, but if you think I'm going to jump into a tub full of dog-food slush, you're beyond whack!"

A basket full of holly-shaped bookmarks fluttered over the carpet. A second pile of books teetered in the air, ready to follow.

A little kid screamed in his stroller. People browsing looked over our way.

"Alyssa!" I yelled.

"How is she doing that? Why can we see the books?" Jody clasped her hands in ecstasy. "This is amazing! Astounding! Wonderful!"

Before I could explain, the books slammed to the ground, hammering my toes. I hopped up and down, biting my lip not to cry. We heard angry feet stomp across the floor. After a second of amazed silence, the clamor of catastrophe broke out all around us. I spotted Hubert's yellow vest weaving through the crowd, but I wasn't waiting around. Jody and I took one look at each other and pelted for the doors.

21 • *Now What?*

*O*utside on Broadway, we ducked around the corner and leaned against the brick wall of the store, panting. It took me a minute to realize that Jody was raving on about the fantastic leap in scientific knowledge that we'd just witnessed.

"Jody," I explained, "she's wearing gloves. Medical gloves. It happened last night for the first time. The latex somehow prevents the disappearing effect from passing through."

Jody closed her eyes and swayed gently back and forth as if she was thinking really hard. I scanned the crowded Saturday-afternoon street.

"Alyssa?" I said loudly. "Alyssa?"

Jody opened her eyes.

"We have to find Alyssa," I said.

The glass doors of Barnes & Noble swung open. Hubert and Jean-Pierre came out and looked around. They began to walk in the wrong direction.

"Hubert!" I shouted. "Over here!"

Hubert and Jean-Pierre turned abruptly and started to jog toward us when suddenly— *bam!*—Jean-Pierre collided with thin air and staggered to one side, holding his forehead.

"I guess we know where Alyssa is," said Jody, jogging toward them.

Hubert was inspecting Jean-Pierre's temple.

"Nice egg." He scraped a mittenful of snow

off the hood of a parked car and held it against the bump.

My heart went soft. I loved that side of Hubert, the motherly-make-you-feel-better side. He was such a good friend. It made me wonder for a second whether he thought I was a good friend, too.

Jean-Pierre was trying to figure out what had hit him. "The lamppost?" he said, looking around in a daze. "The mailbox?"

"Alyssa?" I whispered. I thought I heard crying and followed the sound to a doorway, under an awning. I stopped, put my hand out, and found a sleeve and an arm and a shoulder.

"He's okay," I said.

She gulped.

"He's a boy, after all," I went on. "His head was swollen anyway."

No answer.

"That was a joke."

"Ha-ha."

"Are you hurt, too?"

Jody came over to me. We heard Alyssa sniff.

"Do you need a tissue?" Jody pulled a Starbucks napkin out of her pocket. I heard Alyssa reach out, and it floated up in the air.

"Take off those stupid gloves!" I hissed. She dropped the napkin on the ground. I heard her peel off the gloves with a little grunt, and I felt a clammy wad being pressed into my hand.

"Okay, now what?" I said, stuffing the gloves into my coat pocket.

"Are you all right?" Jody asked.

"What do you think?" said Alyssa in a wobbly voice. "If you think I woke up yesterday hoping to turn into absolutely nothing so that I could soak in dog food, then I guess you'd say I was all right."

"Who's the kid you plowed into?" asked Jody.

"He's a boy from school—" I began.

"And I don't want him to know!" moaned Alyssa. "About the—uck! Billie, I've never asked you for a favor before, but if he hears one hint that I had to swim in a tub full of dog-food muck, he'll never like me!"

"We're sworn to secrecy," said Jody. "If you are."

"Oh, I promise," said Alyssa. "I totally swear."

Wow, I thought. If she likes Jean-Pierre enough to take a vow of silence, I better do what I can to help out.

"And speaking of tubs," said Jody. "What do we do now?"

"Let's go to my dad's," I said, suddenly inspired.

"Your dad's?" said Jody.

"It's only a few blocks away. I have to go there anyway. And the bathtub is in perfect working order."

22 • *At My Dad's*

The doorman at my father's building was a little worried about giving me the key to the apartment and letting me go up while my dad was out.

"Does your father know you're having a party?" he asked. "He didn't tell me you were having a party."

"Octavio," I said, "don't worry so much. My dad'll be home in a few minutes. We just

got here early. My mom's bringing Jane at two
o'clock."

Octavio was also worried about four people
squeezing into the fridge-sized elevator. Good
thing he didn't know there were really five of us.
I was practically hugging Alyssa all the way to
the eleventh floor.

Inside my dad's, we took off our coats and
piled them on top of the umbrella stand. Then
Jody looked at me. Jean-Pierre looked at me.
Hubert looked at me. A hot wind swept through
my head.

Okay, I thought, one step at a time . . .
everybody except Jean-Pierre knows what we're
doing here. If Hubert had chewed enough gum,
then the boys could leave.

"Chew, Hubert," I said.

Jody edged toward the hallway.

"I have to use the bathroom, if that's okay."

"Uh, sure, go ahead. Second door on the
left."

"Ahh-li-*sah*!" Jody pretended to sneeze,
signaling her victim. Alyssa brushed past me to
follow.

"Hubert," I said. "Uh, guys, come in and sit down."

They perched on the edge of the sofa like two nervous patients waiting for a doctor.

I heard the pipes squawk as the taps went on in the bathtub. If only I was the one who was invisible! How did I get to be alone in a room with both boys together and all these mixed-up feelings?

I picked up Dad's *Artforum* magazine and flipped through it, trying frantically to think of something to say. Oh, come on! Was I going to talk about modern art? I put the magazine down.

"Billie?" Jody called softly.

I went down the hall, catching a faint whiff of pig slop as the bath filled.

Jody leaned out the bathroom door. "We need the masticated chicle."

"Oh! Oh, yeah. Hubert! Jody needs the—you know . . ."

Hubert bounced up from the sofa, blowing a giant bubble as he went to find his vest. Rather than be alone with Jean-Pierre, I followed Hubert. The gum-filled bag dangled from his hand as he headed down the hallway.

The lock on the bathroom door had been taken off two years ago, after Jane got stuck in there and cried for an hour. Hubert pushed in without thinking. I stumbled in after him. The smell was like rotting garbage doused with stinky aftershave.

"Uck!" We gagged.

Alyssa started to scream.

Jody's eyes met mine for a millisecond. She opened her mouth and pretended that ridiculous squeal was coming from her. Hubert dropped the gooey bag on the bath mat and turned to flee. I turned, too—and tripped over Jean-Pierre, who had followed me down the hall. As I pushed him out the door, I heard the sound of a slap. The screaming stopped with a gasp. I wondered how Jody knew where Alyssa's face was, but I guess she'd just followed the noise.

"Why make a noise like that?" said Jean-Pierre, once again on the sofa. "Jody was not *in* the bath, after all."

But maybe Alyssa was! No wonder she'd screamed! I would have screamed the roof down. Hubert would die if he knew he'd sort of seen Alyssa with no clothes on! I flopped into the big chair and grinned at him.

But Hubert didn't sit down or smile back. "Jody's a bit weird," he said, answering J. P.

"Maybe she always yodels in the bathroom," I said, giggling.

"You just better hope she's quick about it." Hubert looked at his watch. "I guess we can go now. I've done my part. And isn't your dad coming home soon?"

J. P. jumped up from the couch. "Your father is scary, like your mother?'"

"No!" I said. I grimaced at Hubert so he wouldn't say more.

Jean-Pierre glanced from me to Hubert and back again. He looked embarrassed. "You two probably want to be alone. I was hanging out all this time, and maybe I was in the way?"

"Don't be silly," I said. Hubert was bright pink. Both boys were acting too weird for words. It was time to clear up this mess.

"Hubert?" I said. "May I talk to you for a minute, please?"

"I *am* in the way," said Jean-Pierre. "I should go?"

"No," I said. "Stay here. This will only take a second."

I dragged Hubert by the sleeve into my father's kitchen. "Listen," I whispered. "J. P. has some whack idea that you—that I—that you and me—you know—did you say something to him?"

"No way," said Hubert, examining the handle on the cupboard door.

"Good. I'm glad we got that straight."

"Only . . ." he said.

"Yeah? Only what?"

"Only I don't want to lose you as a friend," he said, stuttering almost. "In case you turned out to like him, I mean, someone, maybe, sometime, better than me."

"Oh, Hubert." I felt a sob of relief tighten my throat. "You're bananas. You're my best friend, forever." I squeezed his arm and dragged him back to the living room.

Jean-Pierre took one look at us and turned toward the door. "I'm in the way," he said. "I think it's best if I just disappear."

"No, no!" I said, grabbing him. "*Please* don't disappear!"

"No!" said Hubert. "Anything but that!"

The pause was more than a pause, like holding a breath to get rid of hiccups. And then I burst out laughing.

"This is crazy!" I said. "What are we being so silly for? We're all friends, right?"

And it hit me that we were. *All* friends, I mean.

"You guys had a misunderstanding," I said. "I'm not anybody's girlfriend, and I don't want to be. I like having just-friends. Best just-friends, and new just-friends."

Hubert went crimson, but I kept going, thinking if I talked really fast, it would be over quickly.

"For a while, Jean-Pierre, I thought you were stealing Hubert away from me. And I felt left out. Then it turns out that Hubert thought you were stealing me away from him. But we were both wrong.

"My New Year's resolution was to make a new friend," I added, "and I'm glad it turned out to be you."

Things might have become awkward again except that someone was calling my name.

"Billie?" It was Jody, only her voice sounded weird. "Could you come in here for a sec?"

"What?" I went back down the hall.

She yanked me into the bathroom. Dad's dumb Mickey Mouse shower curtain was pulled across the tub.

"Mmm," I said. "Eau de puppy snack. Where's Alyssa?"

Jody hooked her thumb at Mickey.

"Alyssa?"

The shower curtain inched open. Alyssa was there, wearing her clothes. She was shivering slightly and scowling with black-eyed fury. Her fancy hairstyle was dripping wet with chunks in it—she hadn't rinsed properly. The tub looked like a pig trough. Her pants were rolled up, as if she was wading in a stream.

The odd thing was that from the knees down, she didn't have any legs.

23 · After-Bath Aftermath

Uh-oh," I said.

"That's all you have to say, Miss Brainy Butt?" barked Alyssa.

"I don't get it," said Jody. "It worked perfectly on my dog, Pepper. The new recipe's proportions must be a little different for humans."

"Oh, let's talk recipes," snapped Alyssa. "Like what to do with the pieces of your face when I get through mashing them."

"Hush up, Alyssa!"

"You hush up, Billie. You are such a loser, pulling mean tricks like this."

"I am not a loser, Alyssa Morgan, and don't ever call me that again. I'm saving you, not playing tricks. If you don't believe I'm helping, you can go away now, without legs."

Jody laughed.

"This is not funny," growled Alyssa. "You're all against me."

"Every single person in this apartment is trying to help you," I reminded her. "Jody is the genius who will probably invent the cure for cancer or find out how to breathe underwater or something, and you're treating her like a servant."

Alyssa chewed on her lip, trying to stare me down, but she blinked first.

"Okay," she said quietly. "I get your point."

I'd expected her to bite back as usual. Now it sounded as though she might cry.

"Maybe you're only mean when you're around me," I said. "I've noticed that I'm mostly only nasty around you. Having an enemy turns me into an enemy."

"Heavy," said Jody.

"Can we just fix things?" said Alyssa. "I want to go home."

I was trying to fix things, only she didn't get it. I looked back to where her feet should be. First things first, I told myself.

"This happened to me, too," I said. "Don't you remember, Jody? My hands and feet stayed kind of fuzzy for a while."

"That's what I tried to tell her," said Jody. "Only she wasn't too receptive to incoming data. We need heat, right? Isn't that what we did when it happened to you?"

"My dad doesn't have a hair dryer," I said. "He honestly doesn't have that much hair to dry."

"Let me think," said Jody.

There was a tap on the door.

"Billie?" Hubert whispered. "Your dad just got home!" He opened the door a crack. "He's got Jane with him. She has to use the bathroom."

"She can't come in," I said. "Distract her."

"Your dad invited us to lunch," said Hubert. "J. P. said he'd help make crepes."

"Hubert, we have a little crisis here. Can you think of something brilliant to keep the others away for a few minutes?" I shut the door.

"How about if we blow on her?" I said, getting back to business. "Breath is warm. Wouldn't it have the same effect?"

"Better than putting her feet in the oven." Jody laughed. "Let's try it."

"I wish you wouldn't talk about me as if I'm not here," grumbled Alyssa, climbing out of the tub. "I'm visible again, okay?"

She sat down on the toilet seat, her wet hair flicking drips across her lap.

"Okay," she said. "Let's get this over with."

Jody and I knelt on either side of her and started to blow.

"I can't believe I'm letting you do this," said Alyssa. "It's so humiliating—"

"Shhh." I handed her a towel. "Work on your hair, why don't you."

Jody went for the oscillating-fan technique, using a steady breath and a back-and-forth motion. I tried the hot-spot method, blowing directly on one place at a time. We sat there huffing and puffing for at least two minutes before a shadowy impression of Alyssa's legs shimmered into sight.

"It's working!" said Jody.

"Keep blowing," said Alyssa. "Come on. Faster!"

Slowly, Alyssa's legs began to take shape. Jody and I kept on blowing, working our way down to the ankles.

"Billie!" Jane's voice rang from the hallway.

"Jane, no!" Hubert yelled as the door swung open.

"I have to pee!"

24 • The End

O h, shoot," I said.

"Oh, no!" said Hubert, coming in behind Jane with Jean-Pierre at his side.

"Alyssa!" Jane stared. "Why don't you have any feet?"

"What?" gasped Jean-Pierre.

"Go away," moaned Alyssa.

"How did Alyssa come to be here?" asked Jean-Pierre.

"Can you stand up with no feet?" asked Jane. "I really have to pee."

"Go *away*," said Alyssa.

"Ohmigod," said Hubert.

Jean-Pierre crouched between Jody and me, transfixed. Jody continued to breathe steadily on Alyssa's right foot, which was slowly, slowly reappearing.

"Wow!" said Jean-Pierre. *"Extraordinaire!"*

Alyssa covered her face with her hands—dying, I'm sure, of mortification. She didn't realize Jean-Pierre was fascinated.

"May I try?" He plucked Alyssa's left ankle out of my grasp and took over the blowing operation. Alyssa jerked her leg, nearly kicking him in the chin, but he held on.

"I feel it, but I do not see it!"

"Billie," said Alyssa. "Do something!"

"We all know boys are full of hot air," I said. "So let him use it for a good cause. Think of him as a prince kneeling romantically before you."

"Instead of some weirdo panting on her toes?" asked Jody in a whisper.

Jean-Pierre ignored us and kept blowing. Within minutes, Alyssa was whole again.

"Now, can I *please* have some privacy?" said Jane, plugging her nose and hopping from foot

to foot. Alyssa stood up and grabbed her socks and boots from on top of the laundry hamper. She flounced into the hall just before my father appeared in the doorway.

"What are you all doing in the bathroom? Is this what kids do these days?"

"Dad!"

"Eeew! What's that smell? What *have* you been doing in here?"

"Nothing," I said. "Just an experiment." I noticed Hubert tugging the shower curtain over to hide the junk in the bathtub.

"Well, it stinks! I don't think your mother would approve of this, Billie. Come on, everyone. The party is moving to the living room. *Now*."

He led the way. My friends shuffled out behind him. I yanked the Mickey curtain out of the way and turned on the taps. I rinsed what I could down the drain, but there were huge chunks of yuck that would have to wait. I closed the curtain again and finally gave Jane her private moment.

Alyssa was in the hall, pulling on her socks.

The others had gone ahead, so I waited for her. I had something more to say.

"You know what, Alyssa?" I said to the bent-over back of her head. "I've known you since kindergarten, just like I've known Hubert. But you've never said two nice things to me in eight years. You were always rude to me, and bossy and mean."

She straightened up and looked me in the eye. "I guess that's who I am," she said.

"But it's not," I said. "That's just my point. It's only part of who you are. Because you're also inventive and daring. Even fun to be with sometimes. But it wasn't until you disappeared that the hidden parts of you started to show. Isn't that weird?"

Her mouth slipped into a smile without her noticing.

"I was thinking the same thing about you," she said. "Not that we're ever going to be friends or anything. But you're not as creepy as I thought. You covered up for me, and you were pretty resourceful. Like with Mr. Donaldson. And J. P.'s pj's!" She laughed. "You're funny and sort of clever. You even, you know, sort of handed over J. P."

"He does seem to find your knobby knees pretty appealing, don't you think?"

"Very funny," said Alyssa, pushing past me on her way to the living room. But I could tell she thought so, too.

"Don't say thanks or anything," I called after her, sort of kidding.

"Don't worry, I won't." She was sort of kidding, too.

"Oh, hello, Alyssa," said my father, passing around a tray of ginger ales. "That's right, isn't it? Alyssa? I wasn't sure who that was, lurking in the hall."

"She's our surprise guest," I said. "She just showed up out of nowhere."

"Can you join us for lunch?" asked Dad.

Alyssa actually grinned at me. "Oh sure," she said. "I'm here to stay, whether you like it or not."

Epilogue

We had so much fun during lunch, eating crepes and imitating my father's terrible French, that I almost forgot about the bathtub situation. Until the smell seeped into the living room.

"What *is* that?" asked my dad, starting to his feet. "What were you doing in there, Billie?"

"I'll deal with it," I said, scurrying to the bathroom.

"I'll help," said Alyssa, right behind me. "But we're using these." She giggled and handed over the latex gloves. "They were in your coat pocket."

On the ride home, when I described the mess to Hubert, he plugged his ears and hummed like a dial tone. Amazingly, Alyssa had stayed and helped me till the tub was gleaming. That was truly the most surprising thing that happened all day.

Ever since Alyssa's adventure, Jane has been begging me to "get gone." Though it is often tempting, I have so far managed to resist. But I did give her a big reward for keeping our secret. I made her a pair of fairy wings, using wire hangers and tutu material and a whole tube of silver glitter. She couldn't believe her luck, but I couldn't believe mine either—that she didn't blab the whole story to Mom.

Jody is writing a book, keeping track of all her inventions and their possible benefits to humankind. One of these days she'll be famous, I bet, but first she has to figure out how to keep her ideas from being used by bad guys—and also how to blend the antidotes more aromatically!

Jean-Pierre came with me as Official Tester when I bought Hubert the coolest yo-yo we could find, to replace the one sitting in my mother's office drawer. The yo-yo craze has subsided at school, but Hubert is still determined to conquer a Skin the Cat, and the Glow-Mobilo will definitely help him achieve that goal.

It wouldn't be quite true to say that Alyssa and I are living happily ever after. We certainly aren't friends the way I am with Hubert. But when Mr. Donaldson made us partners for the "Life in a Castle" project, we built a pretty good model of a cloister without pouring glue in each other's hair.

And, once in a while, in the middle of math, maybe, or on line in the cafeteria, she'll look over at me and say, "Remember when Michele was bald?" or "So, what color *are* J. P.'s pj's?" and we'll laugh till it hurts. We share a secret, after all: a memory that's only ours.

Pencil marking in front 15.99

LP 9/23